A Bliss Case

A Bliss Case

A NOVEL BY MICHAEL AARON ROCKLAND

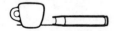

COFFEE HOUSE PRESS :: MINNEAPOLIS :: 1989

_c. 1_

The publisher thanks the following organizations whose support helped make this book possible: The National Endowment for the Arts, a federal agency; The Jerome Foundation; and United Arts.

Coffee House Press books are distributed to trade by CONSORTIUM BOOK SALES AND DISTRIBUTION, 213 East Fourth Street, Saint Paul, Minnesota 55101. Our books are also available through all major library distributors and jobbers, and through most small press distributors, including Bookpeople, Bookslinger, Inland, Pacific Pipeline, and Small Press Distribution. For personal orders, catalogs or other information, write to:
COFFEE HOUSE PRESS
27 NORTH FOURTH STREET, SUITE 400, MINNEAPOLIS, MN 55401.

Library of Congress Cataloging in Publication Data

Rockland, Michael Aaron.
    A bliss case : a novel / by Michael Aaron Rockland
        p.   cm.
        ISBN 0-918273-55-2 : $9.95
    I. Title.
PS3568.0334B55   1989
813'.54–dc20   89-36392
                                               CIP

CONTENTS

*For Kathleen Sarah Ard Rockland
and Joshua Sean Ard Rockland*

I felt as though I were suddenly released from my body. . . .
Knowledge more than human possessed me. . . . I was so happy
that it was pain and I struggled to release myself from it, for I felt
that if it lasted a moment longer I should die; and yet it was such
rapture that I was ready to die rather than forgo it.

Larry Darrell,
in Somerset Maugham's
The Razor's Edge

Everybody always says, Well, man I want to get spiritual, you
know, I want to get heavy. Show me at it. Which way's the mountain and the hammer and nails?

Stephen Gaskin,
Monday Night Class

The saint is succeeded by the revolutionary; the Yogi by the Commissar.

Arthur Koestler,
The Yogi and the Commissar

I

METAMORPHOSIS

Wow. This must be the mystic East.

—Gita Mehta, *Karma Kola*

A middle-aged English professor abandons he family, friends and career to enter a flourishing religious cult in India.

October 1982

How would you feel if you raised up a son and he was handsome, successful, and then, overnight, starts fasting and wearing orange clothes and looking like Mahatma Gandhi? Leaves his position as a university professor? Leaves his wife and children? Goes off to India to find God?

I have nothing against anyone's religion, but the Indians aren't religious; they just sell religion to foreigners. It's a major industry over there. All any Indian wants for himself is a house in the suburbs and a color TV.

I know. Sidney wants to share his new life with me, I go.

But it was so filthy in India I couldn't stand it more than a week. Poisonous-looking green things to eat. Skinny old people sleeping on the sidewalk in diapers.

The trip over doesn't prepare you for India. I locked up the apartment, took a cab to Kennedy, and the next thing I knew I was up in an Air India 747 thinking the country couldn't be that bad, what with the French food, the movie, the lovely stewardesses bringing hot towels.

But the moment the plane door opened in Bombay the air hit me. It was as hot as the hothouse in the botanical gardens, only it didn't smell like roses. I came down the steps of that nice clean plane into piles of garbage and groups of little children, all skin and bones and snot hanging from their noses, holding out hands with twisted fingers and sores all over them.

Maybe I'd have stood it better if Sidney hadn't made me call him by his new name, Swami Anudaba. What kind of name is that: Swami Anudaba?

Sidney said, "Didn't you change your name when you got married? What about Mohammed Ali?"

Look, things were tough enough in India without having to call my own son "Swami Anudaba." Sidney told me I could drop the "Swami" part, but do you know what "Anudaba" means? Can you imagine having to tell people, "This is my son, 'Slave of Slaves?'"

Sidney—I'm not going to call him Anudaba when I don't have to!—was waiting for me at the airport. He was in his orange outfit—clothes, shoes, belt, even this little bag he carried, all orange. At first, I thought he was a lifejacket.

"Dyeing the shoes and belt was the toughest part," he said. Sidney said orange is the color of life, but it hurts my eyes. He also had a locket with a picture of his "Master" around his neck, this soulful Indian with big brown eyes. The locket hung from a long chain of wooden beads called a *mala*. Sidney shyly swung it back and forth as he talked to me.

We went to get my bags. What a mess. Pushing and shoving and screaming. A regular zoo. And, meanwhile, so hot I thought I'd faint dead away on the floor.

Of course, Sidney didn't have any money so I paid for the taxi. We got into the front of this old white Mercedes, a whole Indian family carrying packages got in back, and, loaded to the gills, we headed over the mountains.

All the way the driver never went less than ninety and kept honking the horn. We came screeching around these curves and people and carts scattered.

It was terrifying, but Sidney kept saying, "Wait till we get to the ashram, Mom. You'll love it."

I didn't think so. A mother doesn't raise a child to see him prostrated on the floor in front of King Tut. A son who got the best grades in school. Who got a Ph.D. Who became a professor of English and married a nice girl and lived in a nice house in New Jersey. Sometimes I think that if Jack, my husband, had to die, it's better he died before this.

Maybe we were too liberal with Sidney. Of course, he was easy to spoil; he was such a beautiful child. He had piano lessons for seven years, he went to camp every summer. He even had his own pool table. It was up in the attic and it made him the most popular boy in the neighborhood. His own pool table—and now he has nothing. No job, no family, no house, no nothing. Only this "Master" of his.

"I'm in love with Him," he tells me on the way to the ashram.

"In love with him?" I ask. After all, these days there is more than one Jewish boy who is . . . .

"Nothing like that," he says. "Because I'm in love with Him I can be in love with you." He leans over to give me a big kiss, and the taxi nearly goes off the road.

It's about a hundred miles to the ashram, which is in a city called Boonam, and all along the way there were these wretched people standing around in the fields like they had nowhere to go. The children were naked. Occasionally you saw one squatting in the ditch. Sidney said there are people in India who live their whole lives without once seeing toilet paper. We got stopped in a town by a funeral crossing the road. The body was covered with flowers, with only the bony nose sticking up. They were on their way to burn the corpse at what they call a *ghat.* Beggars surrounded the car. We closed the windows, but then it was stifling.

At last the funeral passed and the driver tried to get the car moving, but the beggars wouldn't get out of the way. The driver pushed them with the bumper like he was plowing snow. It was a miracle no legs got broken.

When we arrived at the ashram it was getting dark. I couldn't see too much, but there were a lot of tropical plants and concrete houses and a wall around the compound. Moist smells rose out of the earth. Creepy things were moving through the night.

Dinner was being served in a large lit-up building which reminded me of mess halls when Jack was in the army during World War II. All the disciples had the same orange uniform and picture of Babadahs around their necks. "Babadahs" is what they call their master. Can you imagine, it means "Lord God!" They had huge portraits of him covering all four walls of the building, like Castro or Mao Tse-tung. No matter where you were he looked at you.

The disciples were mostly Westerners—lots of Americans and plenty of French, Swiss, English, and Germans. Especially Germans. Leave it to the Germans to go to extremes. If it isn't Hitler it's hocus-pocus.

There were also lots of Japanese who, I guess, are more Western than anyone these days. Only a few Indians, and they sat by themselves looking glum. Babadahs doesn't care much for Indians. He thinks they're too Eastern; they don't have egos to get rid of. I understand the Reverend Moon isn't keen on Koreans either.

Sidney kept introducing me to people. All these Europeans with names straight off the menu in an Indian restaurant. Ma Prem Papadam. Swami Chicken Tandouri.

One consolation about this whole thing had been that at least Sidney was a swami, high up in the organization, a somebody. I figured to become a swami he had had to lie down on a bed of nails, charm snakes, go into a trance up in the Himalayas.

But every man in the place was called swami. They kept paging them over the loudspeaker in the dining room. "Will Swami Anand Krishna please pick up the phone and call the Zen Road dispensary?" "Swami Prem Dama, your ride to Bombay is waiting."

Swami means "enlightened one." *Ma,* what they call the women, means "she who has given birth to the earth" or something like that. I could have become a Ma the next day if I'd wanted. All I had to do was "surrender" to Babadahs. It's like Billy Graham. Disciples kept coming up to me while we ate, smiling so broadly I thought their faces would crack. They made this strange gesture—put their hands out in front of them with the palms touching, what they call the *namaste*. In the East, both hands in front means you're peaceful; you aren't going to get somebody with a dagger. "Love," the disciples kept saying to me, "love."

"Ditto," I replied. I passed up the hand thing.

I can't tell you what we ate. It was like the stuff you get in health food stores in the States—beans and sprouts and seeds and stuff. Bird food. After Jack died I did Yoga at the 92nd Street Y and tried to be a vegetarian, but every time I went into the Whole Earth Store, with all that dry food in barrels and people walking around with their own wrinkled paper sacks looking so grim and virtuous and unhappy .... Well, let's just say I failed.

After dinner, Sidney took me to be "processed." I signed papers exonerating the ashram if I got sick or died. I paid food and lodging fees which they called my "contribution." Then I was taken in to see a young English boy, dressed in orange like everyone else, but with a stethoscope besides the mala around his neck. You didn't call him doctor. He was another Swami Something-or-other. "Bend over," he said.

He poked through my hair. "What are you looking for?" I managed to get out, my chin in my neck.

He didn't answer, just picked through my hair the way monkeys examine each other for nits. After a while he said, "Okay, now let's see your pits."

I didn't like this one bit, but I removed my blouse. "Put your arms in the air," he said. He came very close. "You shave," he said.

"I could have told you," I replied. Frowning, he examined my armpits minutely anyway.

"Okay. Hold your hands out in front of you." He looked very closely at my hands.

"What are you looking for now?" I asked.

"Scabies," he replied. I told him I'd never heard of them.

"Okay, now your pubes." Only it sounded like "poobs."

"Why?" I asked.

"Crabs," he said.

Minutes passed with the young man's nose poked into my nether regions. "Turn around," he said. Finally he stood up and said with a reluctant sigh, "You're clean."

After I pulled on my clothes the doctor led me into the next booth, where a very serious young woman counseled me. "We're a gonorrhea-free community," she said proudly.

"You can count on me," I said.

"All residents of the ashram have gone through the incubation period and been tested. You can tell who residents are by the one tan bead on their malas. You may not have sex with them. If you do, they will be required to reenter the eight-day celibacy period and then be retested."

"I'm just here to see my son," I told her.

"Anyone with one orange bead on the mala is a new resident who is in the incubation period or an old resident who is back in the incubation period. Sex with anyone with an orange bead, whether new resident or old, will be cause for dismissal from the ashram for you and that person."

"Orange bead. Check," I said. This young woman didn't believe I had anything on my mind besides having sex with her precious ashramites.

She attached a plastic identification bracelet to my wrist, the same thing they put on you in hospitals in the States, except it was orange. "This identifies you as a visitor," she said. "Visitors are those staying up to ten days. Visitors may have sex only with other visitors."

When I got outside, I noticed my wrist band glowed in the dark. Like fireflies, I thought, wondering if any interested visitors were lurking about.

Sidney was waiting. He hugged me and said, "I'm so glad you're here, Mom." Then he led me up a rickety wooden staircase at the back of a ramshackle building. On each floor we parted sheaves of orange laundry hanging on clothes lines. "Here's my room," Sidney said.

I thought it was his closet. Two skinny, twin mattresses took up the whole floor, and we had to push Sidney's out of the way to open the door. I had to step on Sidney's mattress to get to my own. These mattresses looked like the kind they put you on in dusty hospital courtyards when there's been a major disaster, there are no beds available, and you're going to die anyway. There were no sheets or blankets or pillows—just these wafer-thin orange mattresses.

The walls were also orange. There was even an orange plant growing on the orange window. It was like being inside the juice machine at Orange Julius. The only things that weren't orange were a green lizard plastered to the ceiling like a decal that Sidney told me not to worry about and a lifesize poster of Babadahs on the wall at the foot of the mattresses. I don't know how much I slept that night, what with worrying about the lizard falling on my face and Babadahs staring down at me in the moonlight—not to mention lying next to my forty-five-year-old son for the first time since he was a baby.

When I woke in the morning Sidney had gone out, but Babadahs was still staring down at me. There was no way to get away from that guy.

Soon Sidney was back with some orange clothes for me "so you don't feel conspicuous." I wanted to tell him I would feel more conspicuous *with* the orange clothes but he said, "Hurry. We're all going to Buddha Hall to hear Babadahs." But first I had to shower, as no one was allowed into Babadahs' presence who was not "entirely clean." Apparently, "God" has both allergies and asthma. A piece of lint sets him off.

Sidney gave me an orange towel and some orange soap which he said was "entirely odorless." He warned me not to use shampoo or to put on any cologne or deodorant. "You've got to be natural," he said.

As I came out of the shower, bells were ringing and everyone was rushing through the palms and banana trees towards a huge open-sided building. "Hurry," Sidney whispered.

At the entrance to the building was a fence and gate guarded by these menacing looking disciples who leaned over and sniffed each person, occasionally waving someone away. The rejected ones stood forlornly outside the fence looking in, like concentration camp selectees.

"My mother," Sidney said when it was our turn.

A young, bearded man sniffed me. Then he sniffed me again. "Okay," he said, "but you'd better stay at the rear of the hall."

Sidney seemed considerably relieved he had been able to get me in. "He was being nice because you're my mother," he said. "I didn't get in at all the first few times I came."

At the entrance to Buddha Hall was a sign:

DO NOT APPROACH WITHIN THREE METERS OF THE MASTER. ONLY ONE COUGH IS PERMITTED. IF YOU COUGH MORE THAN ONCE, LEAVE.

Everyone in line was clearing their throats, getting one good hack out before going inside.

In the hall a few disciples were on their hands and knees up front, scrubbing the marble platform and stairs leading to it. They retired and were replaced by some fierce types who sat up there facing the rest of us. Babadahs' bodyguards, The Samurai. You'd see them training around the ashram, doing kung fu or karate or jujitsu—I don't know one from the other.

In the ashram they worry about the Hindus, who say Babadahs is a heretic. Hindus are like Christians—suffering and deprivation is their game. Which is why Gandhi and Mother Theresa have gone over so big in India.

Babadahs is all for wine, women, and song. "Zorba the Buddha" he calls himself. Which is why all these Me-Generation Westerners had shown up here seeking enlightenment.

A month before, a Hindu had stood up during Babadahs' discourse and thrown a knife at him. It fell short and they hustled the Hindu out of there. After that they started up The Samurai. Sidney was hoping to become a member, though I thought he'd have to gain some weight first.

There must have been a thousand young people sitting in front of us now on the stone floor in what they call the lotus position. Try it sometime if you feel guilty about something. You twist your feet over each other. Then you draw up your knees. Don't ask me what's spiritual about it. If I had stayed in that position fifteen minutes I'd have been crippled for life. They'd have needed a crane to get me out of Buddha Hall.

Now a couple of galoots carried in a chair and placed it on the platform like a throne. Everyone was buzzing: Babadahs' chair, almost the big cheese himself.

They took off the dust cover. Underneath was an ugly, speckled thing, an overly upholstered La-Z-Boy. Maybe it was the best they could get in India, but I've seen better in garage sales.

Still, that chair looked like an oasis of comfort. I could just see easing my tush down into it, luxuriating in it. Smart man that Babadahs. Gets the only seat in the house.

Ten young women began to dance in front of the platform accompanied by a little band to the side that tapped finger cymbals and banged sticks. The dancers waved their arms and tossed their long hair. "Sufi dancing," Sidney whispered, swaying to the music. "Getting up the energy level."

That's one of the big words at the ashram: energy. People never say yes, they say "I have a lot of energy for that." Or if they don't want to do something they say, "I don't have any energy for that." Energy happens to them or it doesn't. If they don't have energy for something it never occurs to them that the remedy might be a swift kick in the rear.

The thing I noticed right away about the dancers was their underarms. Regular bushes under there. Even way back I could see they didn't shave their legs either. Like they'd strolled through fields of Brillo and it had stuck to them in tufts.

Pretty soon the dancing stopped and everyone went into a gigantic Om. They're sitting there with their eyes closed making this Om sound that goes on and on. It started soft but got louder and louder until it sounded like the lion house in the Central Park Zoo. Om. The rafters of the building vibrated. Paint chips wafted down from the ceiling.

Try it sometime. Just sit there going Om, not knowing whether it's ever going to stop. First it's scary, but then it's so boring you could scream. I kept peeking at Sidney for a sign it was going to end. Om. All these young people from America and Europe, who could be having careers and making babies, sitting around by the hour on a stone floor in India going Om.

I don't know how long the Om went on before it suddenly stopped. It was as if an orchestra leader had made the sign for "cut." There was an awesome silence. Then a white Rolls-Royce pulled up outside and in came the man himself, preceded by a pretty young woman with glassy eyes who, they say, takes care of his "temporal needs."

People around me made little cries of joy. A woman whispered, "The beloved one." Even I was affected. This Babadahs business may be a lot of hooey, but when you're there, and everyone acts like God walked in the room, you think so a little too.

Babadahs wore an ankle-length white robe and sandals — the only one in the place not in orange. He walked forward very slowly, his hands in front of him in the namaste. When he reached the steps he hiked up his robe with one hand, keeping the other in front of him. Once up the steps he brought his hands together again.

Babadahs stood on the platform now, giving the namaste in all directions. The young woman prostrated herself at his feet, her forehead on the floor. Babadahs is bald and shiny with a long beard. He has these incredible brown hands — long thin fingers and nails which look like they get manicured hourly. I wouldn't call him handsome but he has a curious beauty. He could be smiling, it's hard to say. He looks absolutely blank, like a Buddha.

Once I visited Japan with Jack; he wanted me to see where he'd been just after the war. We went to the town of Kamakura, where the Great Buddha sits. Its a huge thing — so big you can get inside it, like the Statue of Liberty. Except she's tall and svelte compared to the Great Buddha, who's the world's biggest beach ball.

The Buddha isn't all holy and goody-goody like saints. On his face is all this love, but all this cruelty too, like he's sneering at you. That's the way Babadahs looked to me.

His disciples, though, take him only one way. Everyone around me was smiling at Babadahs. Some even laughed. "Ha, ha, ha, ha, ha."

"Why are they laughing?" I asked Sidney.

"Shhh," he said. "I think He's looking at us."

"That's ridiculous," I said. "There's a thousand people here. Why would he be looking at us?"

"Shhh," he repeated. "He looks at everybody. He knows . . . ."

Next, the man sits down in the upholstered chair. He just sits there, his liquid eyes, the color of lentil soup, half tipped up into his head. It's like he's trying to see his own brain. It's so quiet you can hear the birds and monkeys chattering in the trees outside and the far-off whistle of a train coming around a bend in the mountains.

"Have you ever seen anyone so alive?" Sidney whispers.

I didn't say this to Sidney, but that Babadahs, who they say is only forty-eight, looked like he belonged in intensive care. He was beaming and beautiful and scary, but at the same time he looked old enough to be my father, older than Moses. Being a guru must not be too healthy a profession. I thought to myself: a good steak and a few trips to my exercise club on West 53rd Street, he'd give up this monkey business.

The young woman handed Babadahs a lucite clipboard which he held with the ends of his fingers like a precious document. He read aloud a question submitted in advance by one of the disciples and answered it in this high, thin voice, lisping after every word and pausing between each sentence as if out of breath. Was this the allergies or the asthma?

"Anand Deva," he said, like a schoolteacher scolding a child. I looked around trying to figure out who in that multitude was poor old Anand Deva. "Anand Deva, you must know by now zat ever teeng ees holy. Ever teeng piple do ees holy. Even ze alcoholic ees holy. Even ze child molester ees holy. Even ze morderer ees holy. Dees are perversions, bot dey are steel holy."

"You ask, 'How can I be holy?' Bot eef ever teeng ees holy zen ze way to be holy ees to realize zat you already are. Dere ees no udder way."

He went on like this, maybe for an hour. "You already are holy. Dere ees no udder way." I didn't listen to too much of it because I was suffering from sleep deprivation and that guy was a regular sandman. I kept stifling yawns, wondering how many yawns got you thrown out if two coughs did the trick.

Babadahs read another question aloud. "I am sorree, Sangaduli," he responded, "eef you do not know how to yust be. Why should you not know how to yust be? Rucks know how to yust be. Trees know how to yust be. Are you not as smart as ze rucks and ze trees?" I started to nod off.

"Yes, zat ees ze trouble. You are too 'smart.' Your mind gets in ze way. A baby knows how to yust be. How ees eet zat piple forget how to yust be? Zees ees a turrible tragedy. Do you teenk eef man could yust be dere would be atomic bumbs? I am here to teach you how to yust be. I am here to teach you how to do nozing. Udders say, 'Don't yust seet dere; do somezing,' but I say, 'Don't yust do somezing; seet dere.'"

I wasn't sure about the murderers and child molesters, but learning how to just be made sense. The next thing I know Babadahs isn't there and Sidney is shaking me saying, "Get up, Mom." I was stretched out on the floor, must have fallen asleep. Sidney kept glancing about at the few people still there and looking embarrassed.

After we got outside, Sidney asked, "What would you like to do now, Mom?" That's Sidney. "Nondirective," he calls it. Let me tell you, my grandchildren could have used a little less nondirection from Sidney. Especially Jane, the one who is interested in Babadahs too. That's something I don't want to talk about. . . .

How was I supposed to know what I wanted to do in an ashram in India? Anyway, it boiled down to two choices: clean toilets or join the Aggression Workshop. Sidney said new people were assigned toilet cleaning to "get them off their egos." Sidney had to clean toilets for two months when he first came. Maybe that's why Babadahs gave him the name Slave of Slaves.

"I had a bigger ego problem than most, being a professor," Sidney said. But his mother had cleaned enough toilets in her life not to have any problem in that department. I chose the Aggression Workshop.

Maybe I should have cleaned toilets. The Aggression Workshop was held in a far-off part of the compound. Perhaps so no one could hear the racket we made—though just outside there was a crowd of disciples dyeing clothes orange in stone tubs. You never saw so much Rit.

The little cement workshop building consisted of one completely padded orange room—floors, walls, and ceiling—a regular orange cocoon. I was so sick of orange I thought I'd have no trouble being aggressive.

The leader of the Aggression Workshop, a bearded young man, was a former trainer for the EST who had given up Werner Erhard for Babadahs. He began by calling us all assholes. Let me tell you, I have never been called that before or since! I'm a good sport, but there are limits. "All right, you assholes," he yelled, "do you dig it, do you know it, have you got it, are you *here?*" "Yes," everyone chorused. "All right," he said, "Let's share."

Hands shot up. "Sometimes when I'm alone I pick my nose and

eat it," volunteered one young man. Applause.

"I once was constipated for ten years," a young woman submitted. Wild applause. The more outrageous the revelation the greater the applause. It was a regular *People* magazine in there.

"Okay," the group leader said. "Let's get warmed up now. You assholes ready?"

I raised my hand. "Do you have to call us that?"

"Sure," he replied. "Who but an asshole would come to a session where you're called an asshole?" The group found great merriment in this.

We began with an exercise called "growling." We were supposed to crawl around on our hands and knees and snarl at each other, get primitive. "Grrrrr," we all went. "Grrrrr." Actually, it was kind of fun—snapping and snarling at each other like a pack of dogs—but we were supposed to be serious and not laugh. One young man took it so seriously he would lift his leg as he went by, as if peeing on a tree.

"Really get into it," the leader kept yelling. "Grrrrr. Pick out someone you don't like and growl at that person. Concentrate on the dislike. Bark. No need to hold back in here. Everything's all right in here."

A young woman had her face in mine and was yipping and barking and snapping and snarling. Before I knew it she was trying to bite my neck.

Boy, did I give it to her. They wanted aggression? I'd give them aggression. I snarled and snapped so loud she—you should excuse the expression—turned tail and ran off. I chased her, snarling and snapping to beat the band, and when I had her trapped, why not? I bit her on the behind. That fixed her for a while.

But this was only a warmup. You want to hear more? You won't believe it.

Next the workshop leader suggested we take off all our clothes. Oh boy, I think, here it comes. But other than Sidney, I don't know a soul in India, so what did I have to lose? Besides, at my age how many orgy opportunities do you get?

Wish there'd *been* an orgy. Can you imagine it, all these young people: the girls with nice round bottoms and big breasts and the boys looking silly with their little penises, especially one of them who kept his socks on but had a *schlong* hanging off him like a horse.

Anyway, all these young people and me an old lady you can't tell where my breasts end and my belly begins.

"Okay," says the group leader, "lie on your backs and close your eyes. Let's do some rebirthing." This guy wants us to go back to the moment of our birth and relive it. I'm not sure sometimes what I did last Tuesday, but this guy wants me to relive my birth?

"Get into it," he says. "Feel what it was like to come into the world out of that nice warm place where there were no problems. Where you didn't even have to breathe. Now you're coming down the birth canal. Up ahead there are bright lights. It's cold out there. Someone's slapping you. It hurts. Scream. Scream!"

Everyone's screaming. "Keep screaming," he's yelling. We scream louder. Then we're flopping around on the floor, screaming like the Spanish Inquisition. I don't want the group leader to catch me, so I give a yell once in a while too.

You really get to know a lot about people from their screaming styles. The fellow with the big *schlong* is lying right beside me and he's going "Eeee, Eeee, Eeee" over and over—tiny little screams. On the other side of me is a little woman who has a deep, lusty, agonizing scream. "Agggghhhh!" she goes, like they're torturing her. "Agggghhhh!" She's thrashing about, kicking her feet. She even hit me in the shin but didn't apologize. It only spurred her on. I had to move over or she'd have made me black and blue.

It all reminded me of a Vincent Price movie I once saw called *The Tingler*. It was about this little monster, the size of a lobster, called "The Tingler" that was always getting on people's spines and paralyzing them. The only thing that saved them was screaming at the top of their lungs. Great concern in the deaf-mute community as you can imagine.

That's the way it seemed in the Aggression Workshop with all that screaming going on: everyone was trying to get the Tingler off their backs. "Scream, scream," the leader kept exhorting. "Let it all hang out." Believe me, with all those naked people we didn't need any screaming to let it all hang out.

God knows how long that screaming went on. It was like the Om earlier that day, never a sign it was going to end. I screamed least and still got hoarse.

"Okay, get up," the leader shouted, without letting us catch our breath. "Get up and face each other in a circle. Don't stop screaming." We staggered to our feet and kept screaming across at the people on the other side of the circle. "Okay," he continued, "Who did this to you? Somebody here did it to you? Who was it? Look around. Who did it?"

I wanted to raise my hand and ask, "Did what?" but before I got a chance the young woman whose fanny I'd bitten earlier ran across the circle and started yelling at me, "You did it, you bitch, you're the one!"

"What?" I yelled back. "What are you talking about? I don't even know you."

"You did! You did!" There was no changing her mind about me being responsible for her troubles. She was possessed. She kept screaming at me, and everyone else stopped their screaming and watched. It was embarrassing. I kept thinking, maybe they'll believe her. What if they turn on me? Biting her on the fanny hadn't been such a hot idea after all.

She kept yelling, in a German accent no less, "It's monstrous what you did to me, Adele. All I've wanted, my whole life, was a little love. But I couldn't have that, could I? You had to have it all, didn't you, Adele? You had to take it away from me and keep it for yourself."

This is what she keeps yelling, and I have to stand there bare naked taking it. And my name isn't even Adele. This is what I'd come all the way to India for, to be insulted by a crazy Kraut? I started looking for my clothes.

The group leader came up to me. "You're angry, aren't you?"

"Darn tootin'."

"Tell us about that anger," he said. "Don't keep it in. You feel unjustly accused? Okay, show it. *Be* it. Come on now, what would you like to do?"

"I'd like to give that young woman a sound thrashing," I said. "She needs it bad."

"Okay," says the group leader, and what a criminal mentality that guy was, "Give her that sound thrashing. Go ahead and do it."

Next thing I know, me and the young woman are wrestling on the floor, did you ever hear of anything so stupid? I don't even know how we've gotten there. I have her in what somebody told me later was a half nelson, but she's got her legs twisted around mine and I'm really feeling it in the varicose veins. The others are standing around rooting for one or the other of us. "Give it to her,

Adele!" somebody yells. I'm out of breath but I manage to yell back, "It's Mildred, not Adele. I wish everyone would quit calling me Adele."

My legs are hurting real bad, but now I have the young woman in a full nelson. Here I am, sixty-eight years old and having the first physical fight of my life since a boy tried to wash my face with snow in junior high school. And not doing half bad either, if I do say so myself. Those jazzercise classes I took last year were coming in handy.

But just as I'm getting into it the young woman goes limp and won't fight anymore. She's shaking and I realize she's crying. Sobbing. I let her go, a little afraid it's a ruse, but suddenly she's hugging me and crying and telling me she loves me. One minute she's calling me Adele, the next minute she loves me. I'd have settled for a little common courtesy.

Well, I don't know what else to do, so I hug her back. And pretty soon everyone else in the group is hugging both of us and everyone is sobbing. "That was beautiful," they're all saying. "Beautiful." And they're all crying and laughing and hugging each other and us, and the group leader is beaming. And I'm feeling, well, the whole thing's ridiculous but if it makes them happy, so what?

We put our clothes on and head out into the sun, still hugging. Some of the people were going directly to another workshop called Dynamic Meditation, where they blindfold you and you jump up and down for a half hour yelling "hoo hoo hoo." Others were heading for one called "Be Yourself Right Now." The ashramites couldn't get enough of this stuff. There were so many psychological workshops going on it was like an adult camp where instead of losing weight or working on your tennis you went crazy.

There were sessions on holistic medicine and astrology and tarot card reading and rolfing and alchemy and yoga and acupuncture and magic. The Human Potential Movement wasn't in California any more. It had picked itself up lock, stock, and barrel and gone to India.

The ashramites were always offering advice, always taking my emotional temperature. A woman took me aside and looked into my eyes a long time. I wasn't sure what I was supposed to do; I didn't want to giggle. "Yeah, I thought so," she said finally.

"What?" I said.

"Drink more water. Your kidneys need flushing out."

"How do you know?" I asked, curious. I mean, maybe she was right.

"Your eyes," she said. "Drink more water for a few days and then see if your eyes don't brighten."

I drank water like mad the next few days, the results uncertain. Sometimes I thought my eyes looked murky. Maybe all that water was fogging them over.

On another occasion, a man startled me with, "I just saw your aura!"

"You did?"

"Yes," this man said. "I'd be careful the next week or so. The fourth moon of Pluto is in the ascendancy."

People were forever coming up to me with such statements. One received spiritual and bodily health bulletins by the hour.

"This is the most therapeutic community in the world," Sidney said to me after the Aggression Workshop, as we were walking across the ashram. We passed a class in Tai Chi Chuan: kids from Brooklyn, in India, pretending to be Chinese. In the shade of some banana trees four disciples were lovingly washing one of Babadahs' Rolls Royces with lush white rags and the cleanest soapy water I ever saw. "They're making a meditation out of washing the car," Sidney said.

Sidney told me it was all over the ashram what a great session we had had at the Aggression Workshop. "Everyone's talking about your contribution, Mom," Sidney said, "about what a great disciple you'd make."

"Thanks, but no thanks," I said. A week at an ashram may be more challenging than a week in the Catskills, but who needs the abuse? Besides, I only went there to give Sidney some support—and for some peace of mind: I wanted to know why. Why did Sidney give up everything for this nonsense in India? Where did Jack and I go wrong?

Don't think I didn't try to figure this out before I went to India. I even saw a psychiatrist last year. Ninety-five dollars an hour this Park Avenue psychiatrist, Dr. Cohen, charges me, and it wasn't even a whole hour. I wanted to talk about Sidney but he kept saying, "Sidney isn't the problem, it's your feelings about Sidney."

I go there to talk about my problem, Sidney, and this psychiatrist keeps telling me *I'm* the problem. Big help, let me tell you.

Finally, one day I say to him: "Look, I hope this doesn't bother you, but I can't come here anymore." Me, like a dope, worrying about him when he's charging me an arm and a leg to make me feel worse. I guess you *do* have to be crazy to go to a psychiatrist.

Anyway, Dr. Cohen says, "Let's examine those feelings." What feelings? I'm wondering. "The feelings that you don't want to come here anymore," he tells me.

Now, is that stupid or is that stupid? I go to him because Sidney's become a nut. Then I say I've had enough and he wants to examine the *feelings* behind why I don't want to see him anymore. You can't win with such people. If it was up to that guy I'd still be there in his office at ninety-five per, examining the feelings of why I don't want to go there anymore. Instead, I just didn't go there anymore and guess what? I haven't had any feelings about it ever.

That Dr. Cohen! Do you know why anti-Semites are stupid? They think Jews control the world's money. Jews don't control money, they control psychiatry. From Freud to Cohen they're all psychiatrists. If anti-Semites want to find Jewish conspiracies they should forget about bankers and concentrate on psychiatrists.

When Jews aren't psychiatrists, they're patients. Look at Sidney. He had every therapy known to man: psychoanalysis, group therapy, bioenergetics, primal scream, rolfing. He did Transcendental Meditation. He did EST twice. Sometimes he'd say he was working on his body; other times he was working on his head. And what did all this lead to? What did all this therapy lead to? Babadahs.

My people produce a lot of geniuses, but we have no common sense. Other people have common sense; we have therapy. Jews should be prohibited from having therapy. Let the Catholics have therapy.

There's a young woman in my building, Hannah Seigal, who's been in therapy five years. What's her problem? She can't throw out the *New York Times*. Honest to God. Huge piles of the *Times* accumulate in her closets, under her bed, in the kitchen. Her living room looks like a recycling center. She's a perfectly attractive girl, but she has no boyfriends because of this *New York Times* business.

Men lose interest the moment they set foot in her apartment and see all those newspapers.

I know about this because I heard her crying in the hall outside my apartment. She had just trudged home with all five hundred pages of the Sunday *Times* on her shoulder. She looked like a lady Jesus carrying her cross.

I said to her, "Maybe just don't buy it?" Nothing doing. I volunteered to clean out her apartment. Nothing doing. "I can't just throw the *Times* out," she yells at me. "I've got to get to the bottom of my guilt about it first."

A friend of Jack's, Phil Kahn—you wouldn't believe what a gorgeous guy he was—had a miserable marriage. His wife, Frieda, was always telling him what a lousy lover he was.

For twenty years Phil and Frieda were in therapy. Therapy for him. Therapy for her. Therapy for both of them. Psychoanalysis. Marriage counseling. Sex therapy. They bought marital aids. They did it in clinics with people watching behind mirrors. Every cent of extra income, every cent of savings, poured down the therapy rathole. Finally, Frieda runs off to California with a dentist. Phil, he's so miserable. What's the solution? Grief Therapy now he has to have.

One day, Phil meets this lovely woman. She's mad about him, worships the ground he walks on. She tells him he's the world's greatest lover. Phil can't believe it. Nothing has changed with him, except he's met a woman who likes him the way he is. So he quits the Grief Therapy, marries the woman, and you never saw two people so happy.

Sometimes I think psychotherapy isn't the cure, it's the disease. It's like heroin. You have to quit it, cold turkey, to get better.

I get more out of talking to Elaine about Sidney than I did talking to that nut, Dr. Cohen. The only thing that's wrong with Elaine is she's too good. "Elaine," I always tell her, "you're too good." Of course, maybe if she wasn't so good Sidney wouldn't have walked all over her.

Not that Elaine is responsible for this Babadahs business. Back when Elaine and Sidney got married I was afraid Sidney would become a Protestant. He didn't, thank God, but now look what's happened. It doesn't seem fair to Elaine that she marries a Jew, gets her anti-Semitic family to rally round, and the next thing you know, her Jew is practically a Hindu.

I go out to see Elaine and the kids in New Jersey once a month. They have this old house in Griggstown by the Millstone River, one part eighteenth century the other nineteenth. There's woods and rocks and the river and the canal. Everywhere you go there's a marker about George Washington. George Washington crossed that little stone bridge. George Washington sat under that tree. George Washington slept here, there, and the next place. There are horse farms nearby and a beautiful, white Dutch Reformed church across the road from where they live. It looks more like Vermont than Vermont.

But Elaine says Sidney was never happy there. Actually, she says Sidney was never happy anywhere. "He always wanted something. I never knew what it was."

When I got back from India I waited a few days before going out to Griggstown. I didn't want to bring any diseases along. Naturally, Elaine wanted to know about my experiences with Sidney.

That's the trouble with Elaine: she's stuck on Sidney; she's still hoping he'll come back someday. She keeps his books dusted and in perfect alphabetical order. She hasn't changed anything about the house since he left—hasn't put up any new curtains, hasn't bought anything. Nothing. The house is a museum.

She hasn't even done anything about the wine labels on the kitchen walls. Sidney used to keep racks of good wine down in the cellar. He was very proud of that wine cellar. Every time they drank one of the bottles he would get the label off somehow and glue it to the kitchen wall. Little by little he papered the whole kitchen with those labels. When he left there was only a small empty space over the doorway to the dining room. A dozen labels would have filled it. But the kitchen remains that way to this day—twelve labels short. I said to Elaine, "Why don't you put up twelve more labels—or paint the whole thing over?" She just looked at me and smiled.

Ah, that smile. Most of the time Elaine looks depressed, but when she smiles she lights up the house.

Every time I come over Elaine sits me down with the kids and shows slides. Pictures from twenty years ago, when Sidney was chubby and had a crewcut and the kids were little. Pictures in front of the house, by the treehouse out back, down by the river. I wish she didn't show me those slides. It's like looking at ghosts.

Then Elaine gets out the family photo albums. A university magazine story on Sidney called "The Life of a Typical Professor" is pasted in one album. Out of all those hundreds of professors he was the one they picked for "typical." The story has pictures of Sidney lecturing at the university in a tweed suit; Sidney standing sternly behind Elaine and the children, a pipe in his mouth; Sidney in a cardigan sweater opening a bottle of wine at home. It's like looking at a high school yearbook and realizing that my Sidney, now a swami, was once chosen Most Likely to Succeed.

I've never shown Elaine a picture Sidney sent me from India. Actually, it's a collage of pictures — a xerox of all his old passport pictures laid side by side. In the first picture he's a chubby little kid about to visit Israel at the time of his bar mitzvah. In the second picture he has a crewcut. In the third he has a clipped beard. In the fourth picture he has long hair and a scraggly beard. In the last picture, which is from his current passport, his hair and beard are even longer and he has the Babadahs mala around his neck. At the bottom of the xerox Sidney had scrawled "Metamorphosis."

Why "Metamorphosis"? Isn't that the story about the man who turned into a cockroach? That's not a very attractive way to sum up one's life.

Sometimes I say to Elaine, "Elaine, why don't you forget about Sidney?" But she answers, with that smile of hers, "Forget about him? Why should I forget about him? He's family." "Family," she says, and they've been divorced three years.

All my friends' sons get divorces and they sit on the park benches telling the world they always knew their former daughters-in-law were tramps. I don't get that luxury. I probably like my former daughter-in-law more than my son!

Let me tell you something: Elaine is pretty, she's the world's best cook, she gave him a beautiful home and two lovely children, and what did she get in return? Heartache. Elaine is still burning the candle in the window for Sidney. Did you ever hear of a former mother-in-law hoping a former daughter-in-law can find a nice boy to marry?

Sidney isn't burning any candles in the window in India for Elaine. Sidney's a regular Swami Don Juan. The evening after the Aggression Workshop Sidney says to me, "Mom, where are you going to be during the blackout?"

Every night there's a blackout in the ashram during what they call the "energy darshans." This is when Babadahs has "intensives" with small groups of disciples. Gives them the third eye treatment. Everywhere in the ashram you can hear the music getting louder and louder, and then they turn out the lights for an hour so that, as Sidney says, "Everyone can participate in the energy." Most of the disciples who aren't at the energy darshan spend the blackout talking quietly, dancing about, or they go off "into the bushes."

Sidney always went off into the bushes. After asking where I was going to be during the blackout he said, "I was hoping to have our room free so I could be with someone up there." He put a lot of emphasis on *be*.

Well, I thought to myself, he's divorced and a grown man. He can do what he wants. But I felt a little indecent, knowing Elaine never sees anyone in New Jersey.

Shortly after our conversation I saw Sidney heading towards the room with a wild-haired lady disciple. And every evening after that he asked where I was going to be during the blackout and I said, "Under the trees looking at the monkeys," and that seemed okay with him and later I'd see him heading for the room with one lady or another.

One night I must have come back to the room too soon, even though the lights had been back on half an hour. As I climbed the stairs I could hear them at it. It sounded like someone was being murdered up there. I slunk back down the stairs.

Understand, I'm no prude. Sixty-eight or not, my own adventures aren't over. I could tell you about a time last year in Miami. . . . I just wish Sidney had, well, cut it out for the week I was there. I don't think that was too much to ask.

He seemed aware of my irritation because he said, "Mom, I'm getting bad energy off you about what I do during the blackouts."

"Oh?" I said. I was only going to be there a short time. I didn't want any arguments.

"Babadahs believes if people have all the sex they want, sex assumes the proper place in their lives. There's a lot of celibates here who used to have sex three times a day."

"Three times a day of anything you might get tired of it," I said.

"Now what they're into is cosmic orgasm." I thought of asking what that is but decided it was better not to know.

The next night was Sidney's turn to attend an energy darshan. It scared the daylights out of me.

All day long Sidney had me scrubbing and scrubbing to make sure I could get in. "I want you up front near me, Mom," he said, "and you've got to be perfect or they won't let you in." I washed my clothes out three times. I scrubbed myself so raw I left skin in the shower. I don't know if any of this did any good though. It was so hot, two minutes out of the shower I was sticky again.

Sidney, meanwhile, was working on himself. He'd keep putting this little stick under his fingernails. You never saw such nails. White as baby teeth. And he kept scraping his tongue with something that looked like a tongue depressor. "This is like my wedding day," Sidney said.

After dark we went over to the energy darshan. There were only about fifty of us outside, everyone namasting to beat the band. Nobody made a sound except the sniffers. This time they really gave me the business. My friend Tilly's boxer has never given me such a thorough going-over.

Inside the hall, the twelve disciples there for the "treatment" sat up front, the rest of us, family and friends, a little way back. The disciples arranged themselves in groups of three, sitting on the floor behind each other like a toboggan team. Sidney had told me earlier that, because I was visiting, he was going to be allowed the central position in his group, apparently the most favored.

Soon the musicians filed in and sat off to the side. They started to play softly. Then louder. Babadahs came in like a surgeon entering an operating room. The lights dimmed. The music got still louder. Then ear-splittingly loud, the bongo drums crashing. It was like a Tarzan movie when the natives are about to sacrifice a virgin.

Babadahs touched a switch and the lights went out in the ashram everywhere except for a tiny spot above him and the groups of disciples. He moved towards the first group. One by one he put his thumb in the middle of the disciples' foreheads, "pressing the third eye."

Each disciple reacted differently, but they all had fits. One young man's eyes rolled around in their sockets like loose ball bearings. A woman frothed at the mouth. Another woman's body went limp and then began to flop around like a fish.

When Babadahs turned to Sidney's group I thought: I don't

want to watch this. It worried me more than coming upon him with one of his lady friends. Who wants to watch your own son getting shock therapy?

Sidney was holding the young man in front of him, and the woman behind Sidney was holding Sidney. As Babadahs approached, Sidney smiled like a crazy man.

When Babadahs gave him the thumb treatment, Sidney began to moan. Then he whooped a few times, "Whoop! Whoop! Whoop!" Then his eyes rolled back in his head and he passed out. The woman behind him couldn't hold him anymore and laid him down as Babadahs approached her. Sidney remained that way for the rest of the session, his beard pointing towards the ceiling. I'd keep looking over at him to make sure he was breathing.

Later, Sidney said, "Wasn't that the greatest?" I thought it best not to respond. "I just totally flipped. He touched me and I was gone. I feel so clean, like my life is beginning all over again. I'm a bliss case."

Sidney wanted to go outside and skip. One does strange things away from home, so I skipped a little with Sidney, mother and son holding hands and dodging the banana trees and the couples in the bushes. "Far out," someone called after us.

Close to a heart attack, I sat down with Sidney on the tile veranda of the ashram administration building. The moon was full. "I love Him," Sidney said.

I told him I knew. Then I asked, "But Sidney, what do you want to do with your life?"

"This *is* my life," Sidney said. "All I want to do is be here with Him. I want to crawl up into His lap and hug Him. I want to kiss His eyes. This is my *life*, Mom."

What could I say to such a thing? Remind him about his children? Remind him that he had once been a respected professor? Remind him about Thanksgiving and July 4th and hot dogs and baseball? What hurt was that I'd never seen him so happy.

I thought back on his childhood. What a serious little boy he had been. Almost never smiling. Almost never playing with the other children. By four years old he could read Mother Goose and Robert Louis Stevenson. I don't know who taught him, but he could read! He was a regular phenomenon. The pediatrician said he was an Einstein.

He won a prize for best composition in New York City for someone in fourth grade. Went to City Hall and there was a big ceremony and he received a medal personally from Mayor O'Dwyer. They called his name and he went up there and the mayor gave him the medal and a scroll. I don't know what happened to the scroll but I still have the medal. When I was packing to come over to India I found it in my underwear drawer. Sometimes I think if he hadn't been such a good student he wouldn't be in India now. He went straight through from elementary school to junior high to high school to college to graduate school to being a university professor without once leaving school. Maybe so much school makes you crazy. Now Sidney says, "School is a waste of time. Enlightenment comes through dropping the mind."

Recently I had a phone call from John Rafferty, Sidney's roommate in college. He was in New York and decided to look Sidney up. Hadn't talked with him in fifteen years. When I told him Sidney was in India he said, "Visiting or working?"

He couldn't believe it when I told him what Sidney *was* doing there. "That's incredible," he kept saying. "That's incredible."

John Rafferty said Sidney was the last person imaginable going to India to prostrate himself before a guru. "He's goofing," Rafferty said. "Just wait. He'll come home some day and you'll have a good laugh."

Rafferty asked me for Sidney's address in India and later sent me a copy of the letter he sent him. I have it here. "Dear Sidney," it begins.

> Are you really over there in India dressed in orange and praying all day? You always said religion was for morons. I gave up the church long ago, what's with you?
>
> Do you remember that time we ran stark naked across campus at 3:00 A.M.?

A few months went by and I received a note from Rafferty's roommate enclosing Sidney's response to him. "I bring you greetings in His name," Sidney began. "Phew" said the note from Rafferty to me. "It's as if Sidney decided one day to be someone else."

"What do you hear from your son, Sidney?" neighbors ask. They saw him grow up so, naturally, they're curious. What am I supposed to say? Danny Bickel's son is now attorney general of Kansas. Myrtle Dunsky's daughter is a surgeon. For years I could tell people Sidney was a professor of English at Rutgers University. What do I tell them now? I find myself avoiding people. Mind you, Sidney didn't change overnight. You could see this coming a long way off.

I remember an argument I had with him about my brother Sam. As a boy, Sidney had always liked Sam. Sam didn't have children of his own and often took Sidney fishing or to a Brooklyn Dodgers game. So imagine my surprise when I heard Sidney reprimanding my grandson Harry for something, saying, "You keep doing that, you'll end up like Uncle Sam, selling used cars in the Bronx."

"And what's wrong with selling used cars in the Bronx?" I asked. Later, Sidney started making cracks about me working in advertising.

Then he grew a beard. Clipped short, but it was still a beard. In my day only rabbis and degenerate Frenchmen had beards.

Around that time Sidney got tenure and Elaine inherited that money . . . . Maybe that's the problem: if he hadn't had a guaranteed job and lots of extra money, none of this would have happened.

Sidney stopped getting haircuts and let his beard grow. He wore raggedy jeans and love beads around his neck. He'd go to antinuclear rallies, and he was right about that; but later I heard from Elaine he was smoking marijuana. I guess now everyone does it, but when I was young only Puerto Ricans smoked marijuana.

I'd say to him, "Come on, Sidney, who are you kidding?" He didn't like that one bit. Sometimes he'd stop talking to me months at a time.

Sidney showed up at my apartment in the city one day with a skinny little man in filthy clothes. He was so tiny he was practically a gnome. Sidney said he was an artist and his name was "September 21, 1976" or something like that. I asked the little man, "What do I call you for short?"

He didn't answer. From his back pocket he took out this stack of greasy cards held together by a thick rubberband and started rifling through it. At last, he handed me one of them: "SEPTEMBER WILL DO" it said. He took the card back and replaced it in the stack.

Sidney explained that September 21, 1976 didn't speak.

"You mean he can't?" I asked, imagining the poor fellow had had his tongue cut out or was deaf and dumb.

"No, no," Sidney replied. "He just doesn't. Gave up speaking over a year ago."

I asked Sidney what kind of art the young man did.

"This is it," Sidney said. "Conceptual."

"Oh," I said.

Then it occurred to me that September 21 was that day's date.

"Yes," Sidney explained. "Tomorrow his name will be September 22." I thought of saying "Keeps up to date, eh?" but I didn't want to distract the little man, who was furiously rifling through the stack of cards. He held up one card, shook his head, returned it to the stack, and started looking again.

Minutes went by. I wasn't sure what to do. We were still standing there in the foyer, so I suggested they come into the living room and sit down while the young man searched the stack.

I was glad the dirty little man chose the wing chair, as I was thinking of having it recovered anyway. His legs were so short they didn't reach the floor. He just sat there going through the stack like a child examining a deck of cards. Finally, he smiled and held up a card.

"Don't get up," I said, crossing the living room to look at it. He was so low down I had to bend over and cock my head to one side. The card said:

TODAY'S ART WILL BE NOT ONLY IRRELEVANT TOMORROW;
IT WILL BE DANGEROUS. REMBRANDT IS FASCISM.

I wanted to say to Sidney, Who is this squirt and why did you bring him here? but Sidney seemed to think the dirty little man was some kind of genius.

A few weeks later I received an invitation from Sidney to a two-day art show where September, or whatever his name was by then, was "performing," as Sidney put it. On the invitation was a photograph of the little man sitting naked on a pile of sand.

I like to keep up with things so I went to the opening of the exhibition at a small gallery in SOHO. There, in the middle of the salon, the little man, badly in need of a bath, was sitting stark naked on a pile of sand just like in the picture. He sat there staring straight ahead, without doing or saying anything. He didn't even have his stack of greasy cards. In front of him a tall, wooden clock stood on the floor. There didn't seem to be any art objects to buy, though there was a box labeled "Contributions" at the entrance to the salon. Everyone at the opening walked around the little man and the clock, whispering as they sipped wine and nibbled cheese. Occasionally, someone put money into the contributions box.

Sidney walked about with a large Polaroid camera, taking flash pictures of everyone in the gallery as they looked at the little man. As each photo popped out the bottom of the camera, Sidney attached it to the walls of the gallery with colored pushpins. Soon the walls were covered with these photographs. "I get it," a tall, skinny woman with terrible breath whispered in my face.

At eight the clock began to ring the hour, and when the last bong sounded the little man sprang into action. Beside him in the sand he had secreted little scissors—the kind you cut toenails with—and a stack of tiny plastic containers. The little man cut hairs off his body with the scissors: one from his head, then one from his armpit, then one from his chest, then one from his groin, then one from his legs. Then he did it all over again in the same order. As he cut each hair he placed it in a plastic container and presented it with great ceremony to one of the guests. After this there was a noticeable increase in activity at the contributions box.

As soon as everyone had received a container the little man buried the scissors and remaining containers in the sand and went back to staring straight ahead. Just then a large, fat man bustled into the gallery. "Am I too late?" he asked Sidney.

"You'll have to catch the nine o'clock," Sidney told him.

"But I've got to be at Bertha's opening then," the fat man pleaded.

Sidney told him the exhibition was continuous for forty-eight hours; he could come back on the hour anytime. I always meant to ask Sidney if the exhibition really did keep going for forty-eight hours. Who came to it at four in the morning? When and how did the dirty little man eat and go to the bathroom?

You can imagine how all of this made me worry about Sidney. I don't mean I worried day and night. America was becoming crazier all the time, and Sidney didn't seem that far out of step. Besides, he was a professor. "He must be getting these ideas from his students," I thought.

So I worried but I didn't worry. It's only now, looking back, that

I see him with all these changes moving slowly towards this Baba-dahs business.

The trouble was, along the way I never knew whether to disap-prove entirely, a little, or to keep quiet. Do you tell a forty-year-old son he's acting like a nut? Once I visited the family in Griggstown and Sidney was sitting on the living room floor in a trance. He stayed like that almost an hour before saying hello to me. Everyone in the house had to be quiet during that hour. The kids tiptoed about. Elaine and I sat in the kitchen whispering.

The next time I visited the family Sidney wasn't there at all. "He's at his apartment," Elaine said.

"Do you mean you're . . . separated?" I asked.

"No," Elaine said. It was nothing like that. Sidney needed to be by himself some of the time. He needed "space." He had this apart-ment in New Brunswick near the university with his friend George. "But he comes home weekends," Elaine said, reassuring-ly. I wasn't sure who she was trying to reassure, me or herself.

A few weeks later he stopped coming home weekends regu-larly. "He appears from time to time," Elaine told me over the phone. "He's terribly busy in the Movement."

It turned out Sidney had become a great leader in the women's liberation. He was making speeches everywhere. I even read about him in the *New York Times*.

Here was Elaine lashed to the kitchen and Sidney manning the barricades for women's liberation. I felt I should have a long talk with someone, but I wasn't sure which of them needed it more.

Sidney had a new theory of marriage. "Of course I love Elaine," he told me over the phone. "I just can't stay in Griggstown all the time. That's the house where I never grew up." Sidney used to say the same thing about my house.

I'm not sure when the divorce became inevitable. Elaine never wanted it — maybe because Sidney kept insisting he loved her, he just needed his freedom. Elaine gave it to him the way she gave him everything he asked for. "All I ever wanted was for him to love me," she said.

Sidney didn't even have to support the kids. Elaine had inherited all that money in stocks and cattle out in Nebraska when her grandfather died. Once Sidney joined Babadahs and quit the university he had nothing but a small pension anyway.

It was around then that Sidney appeared at my apartment in the city one day in orange. I knew he'd been to India over the summer but when I answered the door I thought: Oh oh, the Hare Krishnas. There was this Hare Krishna group that hung out — or whatever Hare Krishnas do — on West 79th. With their shaven heads, they'd dance around in these orange robes, hour after hour, banging on their tambourines and chanting "Hare Krishna, Hare Krishna" — you'd think they'd get bored. Usually I would cross the street to avoid them.

So when Sidney appeared in orange at my door my first thought was, "I'll have to talk to the super; the Hare Krishnas are getting into the building." Then I realized, "My God, it's Sidney; he's a Hare Krishna." But he had all his hair — in fact, it was hanging down to his shoulders. He stood there smiling in that maniacal way of his that seems to suggest, "I know something you don't."

I looked at Sidney good and long and said, "So, Sidney, what's this?"

"Anudaba," he said. "My name is Swami Anudaba." Here was my Sidney, who grew up in a good family and went to a good college and had a fine profession and children and responsibilities saying he was "Swami Anudaba."

"It's like being born again," Sidney said, as if that explained everything. Born again, my foot! All those hours of labor I put in forty-two years ago weren't good enough for him?

Well, he came in and had supper and told me all about how his life was different now, that he was happy for the first time, that if I really loved him I would support him in his "new path."

Six months later he returned to India for good. He wrote me regularly from the ashram, told me about this "master" of his. Eventually, I agreed to go see for myself.

And as we sat on the verandah that night after Sidney got jolted by Babadahs and we had skipped around the ashram, I found myself wishing I could just relax and say, like young people these days, "He's doing his thing."

And for a while there, as we sat in the darkness just experiencing the night sounds of India and the warm dew, I felt peaceful. My mind wandered back to when Sidney was a child and I took him to the park and sat on the bench with the other young mothers watching their children play. Sidney always played next to me. My peace evaporated with the rising sun. There was a letter the next day from Elaine, sent to me care of Sidney. The letter said my granddaughter Jane was coming to India. I said I didn't want to talk about this. It's one thing when a grown man throws away his life, but a young girl? Elaine said in the letter, "Mildred, I'm frightened I'm going to lose her too. Please get Sidney to stop influencing her. She's quit college. Lately she's been going to meetings in New York of the orange people."

I had been trying to avoid conflicts with Sidney. Now I had no choice. "Sidney," I said, "You've got to stop Jane from coming over here."

Sidney was interested in nothing of the kind. "My name is Anudaba," he reminded me.

"Anudaba," I said, reluctantly, "she's only eighteen."

"That's lucky," he replied. "She'll have less mind to give up."

From that moment on things weren't the same between Sidney and me in India. I kept mentioning Jane, but Sidney only got angry. "Look," he said, "you're asking me to talk my daughter out of doing the greatest thing she can with her life. Why should I do that?"

To take my mind off things, I volunteered to clean toilets — couldn't take another psychological workshop. From ten to one I cleaned. Then there was a lunch break and I cleaned from two to five, when someone from the kitchen brought around tea. Then one more hour of cleaning.

These weren't toilets so much as holes in the floor. Inside the stall are two tile treads that people stand on to stoop over the hole. What the cleaning was about is that a lot of people missed the hole.

You could flush these toilets, only you had to be careful not to be too close or the water would come rushing up and soak your feet. Basically, you hit the flusher and ran.

I had been trying to use these toilets myself all week with little success. Part of the problem was they were coeducational. I may be the only Westerner in history to visit India and develop constipation.

In addition to cleaning the toilets themselves I had to scrub and clean the walls of the stalls wherever there was graffiti. The graffiti was written with the orange felt tip pens everyone in the ashram has, so it was easy to scrub off the walls. There was a sign in each stall: "Only Felt Tips, Please. Put Date. Old Graffiti Removed Tuesdays."

The graffiti wasn't the perverted stuff like at home. It was all about Babadahs. "He loves you," "He's watching you"—stuff like that. Almost the way people paint "Jesus Saves" on sharp curves alongside American highways. There were also drawings of Babadahs with huge eyeballs. Whenever Babadahs was mentioned, "He" or "Him" or "His" was capitalized.

Cleaning toilets gave me a chance to get around the living areas of the ashram. I would poke into individual rooms to see how people lived. They were all small—cells really. The ashramites fancied themselves as living in a place that was half monastery, half Club Med. "Imagine priests and nuns who swing," Sidney said.

Each room had a few books—almost all by Babadahs. Well, not exactly *by* Babadahs. Everything he says is taped and filmed and put out in books and cassettes. Everything! They distribute these books and audiotapes and videotapes worldwide and make a lot of money for the ashram. There are already a quarter million disciples out there, and they buy every book and tape they can.

The ashram has already published three hundred books, and some of them were in each room. I dipped into those books. That Babadahs sure knows how to talk.

Each book had soulful photographs of Babadahs front and back. He was staring off into the distance or his eyes were closed, meditating. He was dressed in gorgeous gowns and fluffy hats. With his long hair and beard he looked like a cross between a duke and a reggae musician.

Sidney's room is full of Babadahs' books, and he also has a cassette player and lots of Babadahs tapes he listens to. He also writes in his *Babadahs Diary*. This is a fancy book with photographs of Babadahs and quotations from his discourses for each day in the year, plus space to write. Sidney writes in his diary daily with an orange felt tip.

I wondered how Sidney and the others can stand it, all this Babadahs stuff, I mean. Mind you, these disciples are no dummies: They're all ex-professors, ex-movie stars, ex-doctors, ex-rock stars, ex-lawyers, ex-psychiatrists. Especially ex-psychiatrists.

One of the ex-psychiatrists came into his room while I was examining his books — I had just heard some activity in the bathroom down the hall and was thinking I ought to get back there. I asked him, "How come you read nothing but Babadahs?"

Do you know what he answered? "When you've found the truth, why confuse your mind?" This guy used to be a psychiatrist; now he sounds like the Moral Majority.

Occasionally in the rooms I'd come across a non-Babadahs book — but then it was usually about astrology or tarot cards or magic or reincarnation. I picked up a book called *Nine Lives* in which the author told, in each chapter, the story of one of her previous lives and how she came to discover it. These people aren't kidding about reincarnation; they really believe it. Babadahs is supposed to be the reincarnation of Gautama Buddha. Reincarnation is a lot of malarkey to me, though no dumber than heaven and hell.

In every room there were posters of Babadahs on the wall. I was getting mighty tired of looking at his puss you can imagine. Hadn't these people read *1984*?

I asked Sidney about that one time. Here he'd been a professor of literature who made his students read *1984* and had a bumper sticker on his car which said RESIST AUTHORITY, and now he was living in a place run by *the* authority.

"Well," Sidney said, "there's good authority and bad. Babadahs is the only enlightened Master on our planet at this time. Resisting Him would be stupid."

"What about democracy?" I asked.

"This isn't democratic," Sidney admitted, "but neither was Jesus. The master-disciple relationship isn't supposed to be democratic."

Poking around the rooms gave me a chance to meet people. Everyone wanted to know who I was — what this funny old lady was doing here. What did I think about the ashram and about Babadahs?

"He's all right," I'd say noncommittally.

"Aha," they'd say, waiting for more. When I didn't continue they would say, "Are you going to become a disciple?"

"No," I'd say, "it's not for me."

No one believed me. "You'll see," they would say, knowingly.

It was an article of faith in the ashram that once laying eyes on Babadahs or just hearing his voice on a tape or reading one of his books, it was all over; you were in what disciples call "the orange whirlpool."

A pleasant enough Dutch woman, whose name had been Christina Van Damm and was now Ma Prem Something-or-other, told me: "A friend was playing a tape when I visited her. I'd tried every therapy in the world but was always on a misery trip. I heard Babadahs' voice, and that was it: I fell head over heels in love."

Nobody was putting pressure on me, but I felt pressured anyway. It was like the time when I was young and a friend took me to a place on Lake George called Word of the Lord Camp. This friend was so sure she had the answer, she didn't tell me she was taking me to an evangelical camp. We went out there in a motorboat, and when we reached the island all these young people, faces lit with the same maniacal joy as Babadahs' disciples, danced down to the boat singing about Jesus. My friend fell to her knees moaning, and there I was, a Jewish girl, stranded on a Christian island.

That's how the ashram was. Nobody laid trips on me; it was just hard being myself with all these people grinning at me. Like sticking to your diet when everyone else is eating candy.

They say the best defense is a good offense. I didn't have one, so I made one up. Not sure where I got it; maybe from the expression "Neither a borrower nor a lender be." "Neither a guru nor a disciple be," I found myself saying to people.

Pretty good, don't you think? *Neither a guru nor a disciple be.* It sounds like a famous saying.

I first tried it out on a young man from Kansas who had come into the toilet. I don't know what his name was; Swami Salami, something like that.

We talked for a while and then he went into one of the stalls. "Listen," he said, grunting through the closed door. "Babadahs says the main problem with people is that they don't trust their instincts. He says, 'Don't look before you leap.'"

"Oh yeah," I shouted back through the door, "Neither a guru nor a disciple be."

That seemed to fix the young man. He didn't say anything after that.

After a while, I could hear him preparing to come out. He opened the stall door and went outside, not meeting my eyes. My statement seemed to have done him in. But when I went into the stall I saw the real reason he hadn't wanted to meet my eyes: a spectacular miss.

Still, inventing "Neither a guru nor a disciple be" had emboldened me. A plan was hatching in my brain: why not talk to the big cheese himself?

The ashram had a policy that any visitor could "dialogue" they called it with Babadahs before departing. This wasn't in private. It took place at the morning darshan, in front of everyone. And it was all videotaped, audiotaped, and sent around the world in books and tapes.

"How come you want to talk to Babadahs?" Sidney wanted to know. He smelled something was up. But I wasn't going to tell Sidney. He may no longer be a professor, but he's still the most persuasive person I know. I didn't want to give him an opportunity to talk me out of it.

"Don't you want me to talk to him?" I asked.

"Oh sure," he said, but he obviously didn't. Reluctantly, he took me to the office of the Indian woman who administered the whole place so Babadahs could play God. Ashramites call her "The Pope."

I had to wait forever to see her. She was meeting in an adjoining conference room with the ashram chiefs of departments — or "temples" as they call them — food, lodging, security, physical plant, religious matters, legal matters, publications.

"You are allowed one question," Ma Anand Devora said when she finally met with me. "You cannot make a statement, just the question. You must submit the question to me now and, if Babadahs is interested, he will answer you in darshan tomorrow."

Some dialogue. How could I get all I wanted to say into one question — especially since what I really wanted was to get Babadahs to. . . . Convince Sidney Jane shouldn't come? Yes, that was what I wanted.

How could I get Babadahs to do that? Babadahs thinks the whole world should come to his ashram.

But I had nothing to lose by asking a question. It was better than doing nothing.

I was up early the next morning washing. I wasn't going to chance being excluded or having to sit in the back. What a job I did on myself. By the time I finished scrubbing, I was clean as a corpse. Sidney wasn't saying anything, just hanging around and looking at me nervously. He must have been afraid I was going to embarrass him.

The sniffers passed me without incident (I was getting good at this), and I sat right in front.

After the dancing and the music and the Om, Babadahs showed up in one of his Rolls-Royces, a pink one this time. He namasted in all directions with that look on his face: a little love, a little rage — as if he were saying, "Hey I'm the God of love *and* the God of War."

There's everything in that look, some humor too. Babadahs thinks all these disciples coming from the West to worship the ground he walks on is a riot! "Don't you get it? This whole thing's a goof. I'm just something you've created." Babadahs might just be the only person in the ashram who could appreciate "Neither a guru nor a disciple be."

Babadahs sat down and reached for the lucite clipboard. "Babadahs," he breathed into the microphone, reading my question, "you say no one should be a Christian, dey should be a Christ; no one should be a Buddhist, dey should be a Buddha. Bot don't your disciples celebrate your greatness instead of reaching for dere own?"

I hoped the question would embarrass Babadahs and, through him, Sidney. It wouldn't do permanent damage to Sidney's feelings about Babadahs, but it might give him pause about Jane coming over. And an uncertain message from Sidney to Jane would be more discouraging than all the nudging in the world from her grandmother.

"Mildred," Babadahs said, as if he had known me all my life and, therefore, was going to be very patient with me. Sidney stiffened beside me. Babadahs looked at me then and thousands of eyes turned towards me as well.

The color rose into my neck and face as irrepressible as a tide. There *was* something extraordinary about Babadahs. Much as I resisted him, he rattled me.

Zing zing zing, I heard. What was that sound? Like electricity zapping about me.

"Mildred," Babadahs repeated, turning the full power of his eyes on me, "you have been here a week and you must know by now zat I am not on what you in ze West call an ego trip." Around me disciples roared with laughter, as if it did not require mention that Babadahs was incapable of being on an ego trip.
Zing zing zing. There was that sound again. Was it real or in my head?
"No," Babadahs continued, "I am not on an ego trip. I am on an ego*less* trip." More laughter.
Zing zing zing zing zing zing zing zing zing. My cheeks were becoming numb.
"I am yust a shell, a medium. Piple come to me because dey cannot love. Dey surrender to me — and den dey are free. Eet ees a paradox. Dey surrender and *den* dey are free. Free to love themselves. Free to love udders. Eet ees really very simple."
Zing zing zing zing zing zing zing zing zing. It was getting louder.
"You know, don't you, Mildred, how simple eet ees?" he said. Those eyes. He was a sorcerer.
The way he looked at me. No one has ever looked at me so powerfully. And, at the same time, I felt almost as if he did not see me, as if his eyes were not eyes but doors. Doors to a turbulent and frightening world of lightning and swirling clouds and dark mysteries. Of beauties and horrors. I couldn't breathe. My heart was pounding. I was going to faint. It felt like someone was putting an ether cone over my face.
Was this the orange whirlpool? I was perched on a precipice. And the precipice was just beyond Babadahs' eyes.
I was terrified, but exhilarated too. Maybe I'd give in, fall off the cliff. Sidney and I could be closer and . . . .
Babadahs should have quit while he was ahead. He said one other thing — and it made me angry, pulled me abruptly back from the edge. He said the time had come for me to become a disciple.
Become a disciple? I was trying to keep Jane from becoming a disciple and Babadahs wanted *me* to become a disciple? He was worse than that psychiatrist, Dr. Cohen.
It ought to be possible to ask a guru a question which he answers without assuming everyone in the world is just hustling and clamoring to become his disciple.
For all I know Babadahs is God, but he sure lacks something.

Call it humility. No, call it humanity. Whichever, he sure wasn't interested in my becoming a disciple for my sake. Babadahs *is* on an ego trip.

Babadahs said something then about how my question came out of the mind. Well, of course my question came out of the mind. That's where us plain folks do our thinking, Babadahs. Sure it's great sometimes not to look before you leap, just let go. But the person who *never* looks before she leaps is eventually going to kill herself. How does she know whether she's leaping into the arms of God or Hitler? It isn't as simple as you make it, Babadahs.

Later, I talked to Sidney about what had happened at the darshan. It was clear I had failed to raise doubts in his mind about Jane coming to India. Neither my question nor Babadahs' response had put Babadahs in a bad light. Sidney was only delighted I hadn't shamed him in front of his master and fellow disciples.

But if I had lost the war, I was still capable of guerilla action.

The next day Sidney put me in a taxi bound for Bombay, where I would board the plane for America. Before we said goodbye, he asked, putting his arm around me and kissing me on the cheek, "So what do you think?"

"About what?" I asked.

"About all this. About Babadahs."

"Well," I said, "he's a pretty powerful man, but he isn't for me."

"Why not?" Sidney insisted, looking disappointed.

"Because I already have a guru."

"Really?" he asked, a look of amazement on his face. "Who?"

"You're looking at her," I said.

I I

EDGE CITY

He's a man who loves to play a very dangerous game with life. He loves to go right to the edge, and not quite go over.

description of artist Andrew Wyeth

I WONDERED WHAT Elaine wanted. Elaine always wants something, you can count on that. "A letter from India," she breathed. "Best not to discuss it over the phone."

I bet it could be discussed over the phone. Elaine just wanted an excuse to come to Hickman Hall.

Wish I'd told her I wasn't going to be in the office. I don't need Elaine sucking around here with her problems.

Everybody says what a bastard Anudaba was to leave Elaine. Listen, if I'd still been into women then, I'd have left her too.

People are always on Anudaba's case. When it isn't Elaine, it's quitting the university; when it isn't quitting the university, it's becoming a disciple; when it isn't becoming a disciple, it's the name. "Anudaba," they say with disgust. They didn't know respectable, uptight "Sidney." They haven't, as I have, watched him slowly go sane.

"What an asshole Kantor is," these people say; big investment there in Anudaba being an asshole. After all, they don't wake up one day and decide to be someone else. They don't go marching off to India. They don't fuck anybody they crave. Anudaba has got to be an asshole because, if he isn't, guess who is?

They're jealous of him. *I'm* jealous of Anudaba, and I'm his friend. The trouble with other people, the trouble with me, we fantasize; Anudaba *does*. I was even interested in Babadahs before he was, but I'm still doing time here in New Jersey and Anudaba is in India.

Give the guy credit; he puts his money where his mouth is. Babadahs is it? *Poof*, off Anudaba sails for edge city.

Anudaba is like Christopher Columbus. Maybe he'll fall off the earth some day. But maybe, just maybe, he'll discover it's round.

Wouldn't totally surprise me. He's a powerful character, full of magnetism. Sure he went off to India to fall at the feet of a guru, but at Rutgers *he* was the guru. The students thought he walked on water.

So did I—a little anyway . . . .

And now? Well, this'll sound awful but when it comes to Anudaba, I cover my bets. He sends damp little letters from India full of haiku poems and drawings in colored pencils. I've got one framed on the wall at home, but I don't circulate them in the department. I used to be a messenger between Anudaba and the rest of the English department, but now that he's gone, well, nothing's stopping me from making full professor. Nothing. Colleagues say, "Heard from your orange friend?" and I say, "Huh?"

But I'm no fink. I was there for him after he flipped out, and later, when he went orange, I was the only one who called him Anudaba without his having to beg. He's brilliant, maybe a little crazy, but if he turns out to be famous—I mean real famous: Vincent van Gogh-famous, Jesus Christ-famous—there's going to be lots of scholars and reporters nosing around here and I'll be the one they'll want to talk to. I'll be the only one in the English department who ends up more than a philistine footnote in his life.

Let me tell you, life is a balancing act sometimes.

I guess that's what I am, a balancer. I'm a balancer and Anudaba is a pendulum. I do okay. Anudaba is either going to win big or fall on his ass.

When I was growing up everybody said I was "well-rounded." In high school I was captain of the basketball team and senior class president. Girls? I had *all* the girls. Nobody knew I was a faggot. Even I didn't know I was a faggot.

I guess I'm still well-rounded in my queer way; I stay out of trouble. I may not end up a big winner, but one thing's sure: George Phelps Smith is no loser either, no sir.

Look, I'm no mediocrity. If there was something I thought was it, really it, I'd go for it, same as Anudaba. It just hasn't come my way yet, that's all. Life isn't that simple. Anudaba may think it is, but it isn't.

Sometimes Anudaba's "virtue" is a bit hard to take, you know. Sometimes he really pisses me off, you know. Goddammit, Anudaba, who elected you saint? Goddammit, Anudaba, why do I always have to play by the rules and you don't? Goddammit, Anudaba, I don't think you ever knew it, ever even sensed it, years ago when I was in love with you.

As I waited for Elaine in my office I was down the hall from what was Anudaba's office. There should be a museum the things that went on there; a plaque at least. But Nell Blimpy, who does Shakespeare, has the office now and there isn't a trace of Anudaba. Room 303 looks like any other faculty office in the Flashcube now: burned out.

"The Flashcube" is what Rutgers students call Hickman Hall. It's a squat, glass tower, modern (meaning the windows won't open). Hickman looks like it could give you cancer. They tried to grow ivy on the building, make it look, you know, "academic," but the ivy all died. Hickman makes you think of a section of the New Jersey Turnpike stood on end or the world's biggest dental group.

But when Anudaba was here we were always having to evacuate the building because of the bomb threats; or Anudaba's students, faces painted green and purple, would maumau you in the halls with their guerilla theatre. One time they nailed a dead fish to the English department door. Things happened in Hickman then, and they always had something to do with Anudaba.

Not when he first came, of course. When he first came to Rutgers out of graduate school he actually had a crewcut. Smoked a pipe, the whole bit. He had these English country scenes on the walls and an Amherst College coffee cup on his desk full of freshly sharpened pencils. He wore the right tweeds, subscribed to the right journals, made the right learned remarks. He'd go to academic conventions and American lit types would say, "Here's Sidney Kantor, the Whitman man." Anudaba wouldn't blink; he had his little racket same as everybody else. Even more than me he was your standard academic prick.

It wasn't until after he flipped out that he dropped all that, became the campus wacko, stopped shaving, let his hair grow down to his shoulders, started wearing a red bandana on his head like a pirate.

This wasn't a sixties thing. Anudaba had missed the sixties getting tenure and he was making up for it in the seventies. He had a lot of guilt about not being in the thick of things in the sixties. So in the seventies, as the country quieted down, as radicals became stockbrokers, Anudaba went further and further out.

You'd see it in his office. The English prints were replaced by supergraphics; the supergraphics were replaced by tapestries. Then Anudaba got rid of his desk and chair, put big pillows on the floor. When you went into his office you took off your shoes and sat on the pillows. "Far out," the students said.

Finally, Anudaba went orange. He put up a huge poster of Babadahs and, one weekend, came into the office and painted his door. "Stinking cultist," muttered Freeman Crocker, our chairman, when he got off the elevator Monday morning and saw the orange door.

By then our colleagues hated Anudaba's office as much as they hated Anudaba. They didn't like Ravi Shankar (the "one note -Indian" Freeman Crocker called him) droning on the tiny Panasonic Anudaba kept on his bookcase. And even with the door closed you could smell the dope down the hall.

Or I could. Jack Watt, who does Old English, said to me, "I have nothing against Hindus, but does he have to burn incense in the office?"

It's like there were two countries on the third floor of Hickman Hall. The rest of us booked ten-minute appointments with our students and sat behind our desks wearing coat and tie, discussing footnotes. Anudaba sat cross-legged on the floor talking endlessly with whomever dropped by about Life!

I lived in both countries—maybe on the frontier. Or I was an ambassador between them; better yet, a double agent. On the one hand, English was depending on good old sensible George to keep an eye on Anudaba; it was an unofficial little duty of mine. On the other hand, sometimes when I knew Anudaba was smoking, I'd go down the hall and he'd give me a hit.

Not that getting into his office was easy. Anudaba's students filled the hall waiting to see him, and although *he* didn't care if students knew he smoked dope, *I* did. I'd keep going away and coming back; it was a pain.

Sometimes when I went looking for Anudaba he'd be outside Hickman, holding office hours under a tree. Twenty-five students sitting around real quiet with him on the grass, and every once in a while he'd mumble something and the students would say "Heavy."

All those students is what kept things cool for Anudaba in the English department so long. If you've got the enrollments, if you're pulling in the majors, they can't touch you.

Of course, now I know how he pulled in some of those majors. After he went to India for good, Mary Jane Pauley, this blond, freckled student from Iowa, came to see me, all broken up. "Has he really gone?" she asked, starting to cry. Mary Jane got involved with Anudaba when she came to the English department one day to discuss her major. "Nobody was in their office but him, so I walked in and the first thing he said was, 'What do you think of relationships between professors and students? I'm opposed to them, aren't you?'"

Anudaba was so outrageous with the students there was graffiti about him in the bathrooms, like he was a rock star. It was a bit much. You'd be sitting on the can and look up and there on the cubicle wall, amidst the perverted drawings, it said things like SIDNEY KANTOR SUPERSTAR or ask sidney. And these were just the ones in the men's room. In all my years at Rutgers I've inspired graffiti exactly once and it said PROFESSOR SMITH SUCKS. I've never been sure how they meant it.

Sometimes Anudaba's popularity could be a trifle irritating. I mean, you'd see all these students in the hall and you'd ask, "Whom are you waiting to see?" and they'd always say, "Sidney," "I'm waiting to see Sidney." There almost never was anyone waiting to see Professor Smith.

Anudaba told his students to call him by his first name; he wanted to break down barriers. He'd rail about how students were an oppressed class, the "niggers" of the university. "If they're so oppressed," I'd say, "why don't you share your paycheck with them?" He actually thought about that for a while.

I'd have had my students call me by my first name too if I thought I could get away with it. Students call you by your first name and, next thing, you're in their pants.

How Anudaba pulled it off so long without getting into trouble still mystifies me. Was it because he was so obvious nobody could believe it? For a long time even I didn't know what to make of these flushed young women forever dashing out of his office into the hall. I thought it had something to do with poetry.

Maybe it's just that he was so flamboyant. He'd wear silk shirts, floppy pants, sandals; later, he went around in gowns like Socrates. He didn't walk; he floated. A dozen student apostles hung on him as he glided across the campus.

Freeman Crocker would say, "I can't stand that fairy another minute."

"Uh huh," I'd reply. Suffice it to say I was not the first faggot to come out of the closet. And I did it during that brief honeymoon period when it was okay. Just my luck that six months later you started hearing about AIDS.

Meanwhile, Anudaba was my decoy. He was so outrageous he ran interference for me. Even so, you'd think people would have been wise to what he was up to with the female students, carrying on as he did in broad daylight.

Out in the corridor, faculty would be hurrying by with loaded briefcases; students would be looking at the bulletin boards or sitting around on piles of bluebooks saying things like, "Whatja get on the final?" And inside. . . . Well, let me tell you how I finally found out.

One day I'm passing 303 and I hear a noise behind the door. It sounded like someone was very sick—even dying. "Ohhh," they kept going. "Ohhh."

"Anudaba," I yelled.

No answer.

"Anudaba, are you all right?" No answer. Just the moaning.

I turned the doorknob, pushed on the door. It didn't budge. It felt like there was a body behind the door. Maybe Anudaba had had a heart attack and slumped against the door; a disaffected student had hit him with an axe, like Trotsky in Mexico.

I pushed a little harder, frantic now. The door opened a crack. Inches in front of me was the face of Ling Po Rizzuto, this beautiful Eurasian English major. At least, I thought it was Ling Po. I wasn't sure, her face being so congested and all.

Just beyond Ling Po I caught a glimpse of Anudaba's gauze shirt and his belt—this rope thing he wore. I'll be a son-of-a-bitch if he wasn't dogging Ling Po; Ling Po, who looked like she grew up in the back room of a Chinese laundry, flat irons hissing on starched sheets, Uncle Lu pressing shirts while Grandma Mai Ti zupped noodles. I guess the Italian part of her had gotten the upper hand. Her face in that doorway was pure Ragu.

Before beating a mortified retreat, I heard Anudaba rasp, none too graciously, as if my being there was my idea, as if I had nothing better to do than hang around his office while he hosed his students, "Dammit, George, can't you see I'm busy?"

Though the next day when I went to his office and said, "Sorry about yesterday," he stared at me. He didn't know what I was talking about.

That's the way he was: he'd blow off real good and then forget about it.

Wish I could do that. I've spent a chunk of my life smoldering about one thing or another, cursing my cowardice and thinking, If only I'd said . . . .

Anyway, not an hour after I'd walked in on Anudaba and Ling Po, there he was up on the altar in Voorhees Chapel, haranguing twelve hundred students and faculty as keynoter at a rally about — well, whatever it was about by then: Vietnam, racism, the bomb, women's liberation — and you could see, right there on the button fly of his flared jeans, this large, shiny spot. I mean it was really shiny, like a big sequin. Especially shiny because of the bright lights of Channel 7, which was covering the rally. Anudaba, freshly dismounted from Ling Po, up there for all the world to see with his pants shining with jism like it was the latest style.

Only nobody paid any attention to that spot except me, not even Ling Po. She sat in the front pew of the chapel, her gorgeous legs drawn up in a modified lotus, smiling up at Anudaba like he was Buddha. I bet the only ones aware of the spot besides me were the Voorhees family, who gave the money for the chapel. The Voorheeses were squirming in their graves.

Anudaba had them squirming pretty regular in those days. In addition to being campus agitator numero uno, there was the Sidney Kantor show Tuesday nights, what came to be called "Tuesday Night Fix."

Every Tuesday night Anudaba held forth in Voorhees Chapel, the campus celebrity. He'd sit on a big pillow like a sultan — though dressed more like a guerilla who'd just come down from the Sierra Maestra where he'd been with Fidel. He was at the edge of the altar, where it cantilevered out over the first few rows like a diving board.

Anudaba would sit there for an hour, microphone in hand, playing with the wire and speaking in a low voice to all those people in the chapel — mostly students, but also street people, artistic hangers-on, hippies, peaceniks, holistic health types, the U.S. 1 Poetry Collective, the Lesbian Coalition — you know, the alternative university.

WRSU, the university radio station, would be there covering Tuesday Night Fix. Just before Anudaba came in you'd hear the kid from WRSU say, "And now, live, from Voorhees Chapel: Tuesday Night Fix." Then Anudaba would come out and people would cheer for two-three minutes. I mean, Tuesday Night Fix was the biggest thing happening in central Jersey. There was actually a Sidney Kantor Fan Club of high school students, with t-shirts and buttons and everything that said, HAD YOUR FIX? People asked Anudaba for autographs.

Tuesday nights Anudaba would sit there in the chapel musing on any subject that came into his head, the more outrageous the better. One time he talked about the end of the nuclear arms race, Carter and Brezhnev smoking dope together. The planet was a stoned place. Flowers gave off more perfume, birds sang sweeter.

Another time he came in, took off his sandals, scratched, and started talking about athlete's foot. "Ever wonder why you get athlete's foot in the spring?" he asked, and went on to talk about athlete's foot and ulcers, how they both get stirred up in the spring because that's when acid rises in people same as sap in trees. "We've got to start paying attention," he said. "Dry feet and less coffee in the spring."

His talks were jazz. He'd lay down a theme, embroider it, and finally, through this thicket of ideas, he'd bring it all back home again with lots of like's and really's and dig it's and you know's and far out's.

And all the while the alternative university types would be hanging on his every word, bopping along to his rhythm, even shouting an occasional "Amen" or "Go get 'em Sidney" like it was the Baptist Revival Hour.

I'd be bopping and shouting with the rest—though sometimes I'd catch myself and stop. I mean, I didn't want anyone thinking I was Anudaba's flunky.

One Tuesday night Anudaba came in, sat down, and said, "Let's not talk tonight. Let's listen." Everybody said "Heavy" and hunkered down for a solid hour of silence. The poor kid from WRSU had to walk up and down the aisle with his microphone, whispering into it from time to time, picking up sighs and coughs.

Anudaba was too much, no question about it. That's probably why we became friends. I was the closest thing the English department had to another nutball, but, let me tell you, strictly second-string.

Faggot or not, I'm straighter than Anudaba by a mile. My new lover, Steven, and I are positively bourgeois. We go shopping. We have friends over. I may be a queer, but I'm a New England, old money, white Anglo-Saxon Protestant queer.

Maybe that's why I've always dug Jewish loonies like Anudaba—they'll try anything. Of course, sometimes Anudaba can be downright ridiculous. When he came back from that first summer in India we were bombed on some good wine in the apartment one evening when he said, "Look, George, we've been friends for a long time. Maybe we should cement our relationship by having sex." Just like that he said it.

I laughed. Years back I'd thought about him a lot. He was dark and graceful and smooth and cute; I'm a klutz and I'm all angles and my skin is so dry it flakes off. He's five-eight, and I'm six-five, the Jolly Pink Giant. Even with the beard he had this almost girlish sweetness about him. I wanted to take care of him.

I'd dream about him. One time I was in Atlanta and went to the gay baths. There was this shallow pool in the center of which was a lifesize statue of a nude male figure with an enormous bronze erection—the patron saint of queers. When you first arrived at the baths you waded out to the statue and touched the cock for good luck. This statue had long hair, a beard, sad eyes. It looked like Jesus—except I remember thinking it looked even more like Anudaba than Jesus, that's how much he was on my mind those days.

Still, what a turnoff years later when Anudaba suddenly suggested sex. I guess he thought he was making an enlightened proposition. "Show me how to do it," he said.

But I wasn't interested in being part of somebody's sexual experiments. Anudaba thought he'd try something he'd never done before, a new ice cream flavor, Tutti Frutti, but this was my life; it was insulting.

Maybe I shouldn't have said, "What makes you think I find you attractive?" because his face fell. Though, to tell the truth, I didn't much anymore. The sun in India had burned deep lines in his face; he was skinny as a stringbean.

As it turned out, it wasn't a problem. When I told him sex wasn't such a good idea, he looked relieved. He was off the hook.

Years before Anudaba had been one of the first people I told I was gay. I was worried about how he'd react.

At first he didn't believe me. "You gay?" he said. "What are you talking about, *gay?* You look like Rock Hudson." Then he thought a while and said, "Okay, so you're gay. I like to fuck women, you like to fuck men."

We'd walk along on campus after that and he'd say, "Mmmm, dig the ass on that lass; like a valentine." And I'd say, "Check that cute boy's buns." We'd laugh together wickedly, two middle-aged lechers with nothing to compete about, supporting each other's habits.

Coming out of the closet with Anudaba was easy because we'd shared a lot. He didn't hear "gay" and endlessly flash to George fucking some dude up the ass. Other people find out you're gay and they think it's what you do twenty-four hours a day, three-hundred-sixty-five days of the year. Nothing on your mind, ever, but being a "pervert."

Anudaba knew me when I was married. We lived next door to them in Griggstown; Sandy and my kids still do. We used to get together, he and Elaine, me and Sandy—and our kids played together down by the canal. They built this treehouse and had a club with secret passwords.

I was a good father; still am. I take Ralph into the city to Knicks or Yankees games almost every week. And I was a good husband too, enjoyed sex with Sandy; I just liked it more with men.

All those years I was married I fantasized about men. Sometimes I'd sneak off to a porno peep show and hang around the glory holes—easier said than done when you're six-five and your pecker's half a foot too high. And when I was catching, not pitching, I'd have to scrinch down so low I'd get a crick in the neck.

But, oh, the secret life! The important thing was not to exchange a word, not to know who was on the other side of that hole, not to get involved. Just a mouth and a cock in the dark, while you fed quarters into the machine and tits flickered on the screen.

It was dark and dirty and dangerous. You couldn't know for sure whether a cock or a .45 was coming through that hole or, going the other way, whether your piece was going into the mouth of a poor sucker like yourself or a madman who would mutilate you. It was the ultimate zipless fuck, more zipless than anything Erica Jong ever dreamed up.

Still, I always felt bad about it. Guilty towards Sandy. Scared of getting the syph. Worried sick they'd find out about me at the university.

One day I said to myself, Fuck it, this is who I am. I like being married and I like sex with guys. So I told Sandy. If she'd bought it I'd be married still.

I don't mean I'm bisexual. Nobody's bisexual, not really. We're all basically attracted to our own sex or the other sex. Once I was talking with an out-of-town guy in a gay bar who blurted out, "You've got to help me. I'm happily married but sometimes I have fantasies about men. What am I?"

And I told him, "You're a perfectly straight, happily married man who sometimes has fantasies about men."

"Thank you, thank you," he said, as if I had saved his life. The guy sends me a Christmas card every year from Kansas City with a picture of his family.

Of course, wouldn't you just know that when I came out of the closet I started fantasizing about women. And now I have lots of women friends — which I didn't when I lived in the straight world.

Sandy's my best. She comes up to New Brunswick and we have lunch. I visit her and the kids and sometimes I stay overnight. We sleep in the same bed, hold each other all night like brother and sister. The only divorces I know of where the man and woman remain friends, one or both of them are gay.

At first, things were tough between Sandy and me. Then she went through a heavy feminist thing, even toyed with lesbianism, maybe trying to punish me. She found out she isn't a lesbian, but she stopped feeling rejected — the he-left-me-for-another-man bit.

Anudaba threw a surprise party for me and Sandy celebrating the end of our marriage. His idea was "Anybody can get married. Divorce takes character."

All our friends came to the party except Elaine. By this time things were pretty tense between her and Anudaba, and she probably thought Sandy and I were bad influences on him. So Anudaba made the party in Hickman Hall.

He got Sandy and me there on a ruse one Saturday night. When we drove into the parking lot the campus was dark and deserted. "You sure this is the right night?" I said to Sandy. Suddenly, the lights blazed on in Hickman, *bonk*. Rock music came on, loud as Yankee Stadium.

Up in the English department offices were a million people, none of our colleagues, thank God—except for Carol Johnson, who was our friend then, the department's token feminist—everyone drunk as skunks. Anudaba had some of his students serving the food and drinks. I remember Ling Po Rizzuto was there that night.

On the secretary's desk was an enormous cake which said: CONGRATULATIONS GEORGE AND SANDY. At first, I was a little angry. Anudaba seemed to be making light of a serious matter. Then I thought: Exactly!

The big event of the evening was this incredible Happening. Anudaba had sneaked our marriage bed out of the house and into Hickman Hall, and he had an electric chain saw from Taylor Rental. "You're crazy," I said. "That bed cost five hundred dollars."

But Sandy and I were so drunk we sawed through the bed anyway, end to end, mattress and all. What a racket that saw made. Wood chips and chunks of mattress flew through the air; the office filled with sawdust. Finally, the bed split and the two halves fell to each side. Everyone cheered. Anudaba got Sandy and me to sign wooden chunks of the bed in ballpoint, and each guest was presented with a chunk, like it was a religious relic or something.

After the party I got the apartment in New Brunswick, a fourth-floor walkup on Church Street. Besides the Episcopal church and my building, there wasn't anything on the street but parking lots.

This was before the yuppies began to arrive. Just outside the university gates, unemployed hispanics stood around in front of defunct soft-drink bottling plants, superfly blacks cruised in pimpmobiles. New Brunswick was a city that had died and gone to the suburbs.

But the old church, with its graveyard of sloping marble tombstones, gave my street some class, and up in the apartment, things seemed reasonably civilized. At night I would look out the window at the city lights and the Raritan River and imagine Paris.

The hard part was the loneliness. I missed Sandy. I missed the kids. Missed my house. Missed Griggstown.

I was so lonely I could hardly get through an evening without somebody in my bed. I would go out cruising down this leafy street on the edge of the campus where all the gays hang out, Seminary Place.

During the day, Seminary Place was like any street on campus. Guys who'd sucked cocks there the night before hurried innocently along with everyone else, arms full of books. At night these same guys leaned against trees in the shadows or drove by slowly in cars, only their parking lights on. Was it the presence of the Dutch Reformed seminary across the street which set off all this lust? "Semenary Place" we called the street.

It's very dark on that street at night; you felt invisible. And I didn't want to be seen — though I probably was because I was always the tallest guy there and also because I recognized people *I* knew: students, faculty, librarians. Half the goddamm university.

Everyone was cool, pretending they were there for other reasons. I carried my briefcase so I could pretend I was on my way to the library.

Sometimes I'd go off with somebody in his car for a quickie. But sex in a car is so awkward you can hardly tell a cock from a gear shift.

Usually I'd want to go back to my apartment. Having someone there made it feel like home. Even so, the next night I'd be out on Seminary Place again, frantic with loneliness.

Anudaba and I had lunch almost every day at school; that helped. One time I told him about Seminary Place. A few nights later, who should come by on Seminary Place in his Volvo but Anudaba? He must have been on his way home from Tuesday Night Fix. He tooted at me where I stood under a tree and drove off. Anudaba was good at getting me to laugh at myself.

Anudaba also invited me out to dinner in Griggstown every week. I liked going, only sometimes there were bad vibes from Elaine. Or even when Elaine was nice it would feel like she was trying to get her hooks into me somehow, trying to get me to influence Anudaba.

Anudaba held me together that year I lived alone; he's some listener. When you talk he stares at you with total intensity, his face real close. Every sad thing you say, he looks sad. Every happy thing you say, he lights up. He listens to you like you're *it;* there's nothing else happening on the planet.

Of course, I've been there for him during his bad times too, like when he flipped out years ago. Almost nobody remembers this. The students recycle every four years — and the faculty? Well, pretty soon Anudaba was giving them so much other grief that going nuts seemed respectable by comparison.

It was just after he got tenure. The book on Whitman had come out and he could have just coasted on that for years; maybe written another book on Whitman and made full professor.

That's what I'm doing. But some professors don't know what to do with themselves when they get tenure. They've made it, now what are they supposed to do? They have to be "great men." So they get depressed or start keeping a bottle in the lower right-hand drawer of their desks. Or they do what Anudaba did.

The first anyone noticed something funny about Anudaba was when the mail started piling up in his box in the English department office. He'd always been real responsible about things like the mail, but now, day after day, the secretary put more mail in his box and he ignored it. The box was overflowing.

I was standing there the afternoon he strode to his box, scooped up its contents, and, without looking at the mail, dumped every bit of it into the wastebasket. As he walked out of the office, the secretary looked over at me and twisted her second finger in her temple, making the sign for crazy.

A few days later we were having one of our Friday departmental faculty meetings. Anudaba never said anything at these meetings or he said safe, predictable things. He was always the good boy. But at this meeting — and that was back when he was still wearing his tweeds, his bow tie, his wingtip shoes — he launched into a whole thing about how we should get rid of the grading system.

Everyone looked over at him. Was he kidding? Get rid of the grading system?

"We're a bunch of fascists here," he said, "don't you see?"

"Wait a minute," Freeman Crocker said. "I resent that."

"Shove it up your ass," Anudaba said.

Nobody could believe it. Sidney Kantor said that? To Freeman Crocker? Was it a joke? It must have been a joke. Yes. Not a very good joke, but a joke, no doubt about it. Ha, ha, ha. We went on with the meeting as if nothing had taken place.

Two weeks later, it happened. We were having another departmental faculty meeting, something about sophomore prerequisites. Anudaba was sitting there doodling on a pad, sighing from time to time. Everyone eyed him nervously.

Suddenly, he stood up and shouted, "I'm not taking another minute of this shit," and ran out the seminar room door and down the Hickman Hall corridor screaming like a banshee.

The whole department ran after him; me, as one of the more agile members, in the lead. "Sidney!" we yelled. "Come back!"

"Bastards!" Anudaba responded, lifting a fire extinguisher out of its glass case and heaving it at us.

It just missed me and clanked down the corridor. You should have seen these English professors, including some old buzzards who can hardly lift their briefcases, hurdling over that thing on their withered shanks.

Anudaba made it to his office just before the pack. He swung the door closed and locked himself in. We could hear him moving furniture against the door, barricading himself. "Sidney," everyone kept calling, but all we heard was this terrible screeching.

Professors aren't long on action. Also, what were we supposed to do, call the cops on our own colleague? If there's one thing you don't do in a university it's mess with academic freedom, even when its only product, sometimes, is batty behavior. Academia is a roving nut ward. Look at me. In the university I lend a certain variety to the offerings, but how far would a middle-aged faggot get in corporate America?

So one reason nobody knew what to do was this lingering doubt that maybe Anudaba's behavior came under "creative." Maybe this was, you know, theatre.

Like, there was this old bird over on the agricultural campus who sat around for years with cruddy coffee cups in which mold and fungus were growing. He'd keep them on the radiator and examine them one by one. If the taxpayers and legislature had known about him they'd have said, "Fire the guy!"

So what happens? It turns out that what's in those coffee cups is a new antibiotic. This old bird isn't crazy at all. Before long he's won the Nobel Prize. Millions are pouring into the university in royalties and they're naming buildings after the guy.

So here were all of Anudaba's colleagues, including me, huddled in the hallway trying to figure out what to do that wouldn't compromise his creativity. We can hear him throwing things around in there. There's a crash, the sound of breaking glass, and

Anudaba's bronze bust of Whitman came sailing through the busted transom and landed at our feet. Jack Watt picked it up, noticing that Whitman's nose was a little dented. Jack tried in vain to reshape the nose and then stood around polishing the bust with his sleeve. We envied him having something to do.

Somebody figured we should call the Campus Patrol "to keep Sidney from hurting himself." Yes, that was a good idea. We weren't interfering; just keeping Anudaba from throwing himself through the window or something.

And we weren't calling the real cops the university has now in the law-and-order eighties; we were calling Campus Patrol. The Campus Patrol were gentle sorts who rode around campus on three-wheeled scooters and horses and, at night, lit the way for students with lanterns.

Pretty soon these two campus patrolmen showed up. They didn't look like they could handle a third grader, much less Anudaba. They were trained to respect professors' idiosyncracies. "Professor Kantor," the campus patrolmen called through the door, sweet as pie.

"Fuck off," Anudaba yelled from inside.

The campus patrolmen got on their walkie-talkies with headquarters. Lots of crackling back and forth. "Ten-four. Roger. Over and out." Exchanges designed to inspire confidence in professors and other civilians.

Meanwhile, the faculty were standing around saying, "No matter what happens, we've got to keep this quiet." The English department already had a reputation for eccentricity. For starters, there was sixty-year-old Nell Blimpy with her miniskirts and purple hair. There was Ana Bannan who sometimes, right in the middle of class, forgets who she is. "Ana Bananas" the students call her. There was Jack Watt, "What Watt," who's half deaf but refuses to wear a hearing aid. And there was me, for crissake.

Five more campus patrolmen arrived, carrying a stretcher, a crowbar, and a straightjacket. "Professor Kantor," they called through the door. No dice. They decided to break down the door.

The campus patrolmen huffed and puffed but they couldn't get the door down. One of them, a guy with a red face and white hair, charged the door but nothing gave, and he sat on the floor holding his shoulder and moaning.

The campus patrolmen decided to crack the door open with the crowbar. That took some doing, but finally they rushed in, the faculty following sheepishly at their heels.

Anudaba was atop his four-drawer file, crouched like a monkey, his arms hanging over the sides. The campus patrolmen pulled him off the file case and onto the floor. "Don't hurt him," Nell Blimpy said, as Anudaba tried to kick a campus patrolman.

They had some time getting Anudaba into the straightjacket. They'd get one arm into the thing but, before they could get the other, Anudaba had worked the first free and was swinging it and kicking out with his legs.

At last, they got him into the straightjacket and onto the stretcher. As they carried him out the door everyone was saying, "See you later, Sidney. Hope you feel better, Sidney."

"Ptuh," went Anudaba, lifting his head and spitting.

A few of us went down to the Hickman Hall parking lot with Anudaba and the campus patrolmen. An ambulance was there, its beacon flashing, and two hundred students stood around asking what was going on. Not much chance of keeping this quiet now.

"Isn't that Professor Kantor?" a student asked.

"Everything's all right," Freeman Crocker said.

I thought that was it for Anudaba. When next I saw him he'd be one of the regular legumes in the state hospital.

But Monday morning he was back in his office like nothing had happened. Incredible. They'd kept him in the hospital only over the weekend, called it an anxiety attack. I get off the elevator and first thing I hear is Anudaba on the phone to Physical Plant, calmly arranging to have his busted transom fixed.

"Of course I'm all right," he said to everyone who asked. And he certainly looked all right. He was expansive, smiled a lot, told stories about "my weekend in the nut ward," about "all the great people I met."

Actually, he seemed better than all right. We had lunch, and I said, "Look, don't shit me. How are you, really?"

To which he replied, "Wasn't that fun the other day?"

"Fun?"

"Look, George," he said, warming to the subject, "haven't you ever wanted, once in your life, just to tell the world to go fuck itself? I mean, what's tenure for?"

"Well," I said, "I'm not sure throwing Whitman busts through transoms is what the university has in mind." Still, it seemed possible Anudaba had had a breakthrough instead of a breakdown He'd certainly gone through something, maybe out the other side.

And now he began to change. His hair changed, his clothing changed, his office changed. He began smoking dope. He began diddling students. He became the campus celebrity.

He seemed full of himself, but quieter, more private. He began reading mystical stuff—Hesse, Castañeda, Watts. He meditated.

This made Elaine angry. Religion was supposed to be *her* thing. Elaine had recently joined the choir of the Dutch Reformed church in Griggstown and taken on a whole scrubbed, Sunday school look.

She played *musica sacra* on the stereo all the time. Vast choruses droning *Ave verum corpus* over and over again in Latin and German, awesome funereal music. It gave you the creeps.

Elaine was smug about that music. I was out in Griggstown listening quietly to some Dylan with Anudaba when Elaine padded into the living room and startled us with, "Can't you play that softer? You know I don't feel well."

Elaine never felt well. That seemed to be her thing. She was always laid up with something, would walk around the house looking morose and sick. When she got her period you knew it because she disappeared for days.

Everyone says "Poor Elaine" as if she were a total innocent in the breakup of their marriage. Anudaba told me he got out of the marriage "because I couldn't stand being a bully anymore. Something about Elaine is saying, 'Hit me, hit me.' It's tough living with a martyr."

A year after my divorce Anudaba moved in with me in New Brunswick, first part-time, then for good.

Elaine came to the apartment one day when he wasn't there. As usual with Elaine, I couldn't figure what she wanted. I gave her some tea and finally deduced I was supposed to talk Anudaba into going home. I asked her if she had asked him herself. No, she hadn't. That's the way Elaine is. She'll never say anything to anyone directly.

I wonder whether her inability to face things straight on had something to do with how Anudaba's kids got conceived. Elaine just kept getting pregnant, even though Anudaba said she used her diaphragm. Sure is strange. Anudaba finally got a vasectomy. He felt rotten about it afterwards.

That afternoon in the apartment Elaine stayed on and on, nursing that cup of tea. I couldn't get rid of her. Maybe she was hoping Anudaba would show up.

When it got dark, I started making noises about the neighborhood not being safe. Elaine got up and looked out the window for a long time. Finally, she picked up her pocketbook and, as she went out the door, said, "Don't tell him I was here."

"Yeah," I said, so she'd keep moving.

I loved it when Anudaba moved into the apartment with me. I'd gotten used to living alone, but it was better having a roommate, somebody to talk to.

Actually, I had more than a roommate. When Anudaba moved in so did half the university — the fringe people, the Tuesday Night Fix crowd. Some of these people — the Eastern Service Workers Union, the Take Back the Night Anti-Rape Coalition, the U.S. 1 Poetry Collective — made our apartment their headquarters. They got their mail there and at any hour of day or night someone would be lugging a typewriter up to our fourth-floor apartment or hand-lettering signs or just hanging around drinking coffee and rapping. The place was always a mess.

Anudaba jumped around like a monkey with these groups. I'd lend a hand so as not to feel awkward but, Jesus, I usually vote Republican.

My social life changed altogether when Anudaba moved in. There were lots of people around, and many of them were so funky, so open to anything, I didn't have to cruise Seminary Street anymore. Late at night we'd sit around, Anudaba holding hands with one of the women from Take Back the Night, me holding hands with my latest flame. Real cozy. Sometimes one or the other of us would go into the bedroom with his friend and go at it.

Anudaba never worried what people thought about him living with someone gay; you have to give him credit. He even marched with me in the Gay Pride parade in New York, carrying a home-made sign saying HONORARY GAY.

My gayness was nothing special at the men's group we organized in the Church Street apartment after Anudaba moved in. Everyone in that group was going through a heavy scene. Like one guy, a math professor, became impotent when his wife fell in love with a butch math professor at Princeton. It wasn't clear whether he was bothered most by the impotence, his wife's lesbianism, or her carrying on with someone at a more prestigious university. Who says men don't cry?

Anudaba was the catalyst of the group. He prodded everyone into talking by revealing outrageous things about himself. He'd say things like, "Anyone ever jerk off six times in one day? Why not?"

He was awful. He didn't care what he said about himself, just so the rest of us coughed up something equally gross.

The grossest thing any of the others could cough up, they thought, were their homosexual fantasies or their piddling little gay adventures. They'd look to me for approval; I was supposed to tell them how terrific they were for revealing these dark truths about themselves. "Nuts," I'd tell them. "I'm not the house queer."

The group would get on my case about having been a basketball star, saying, "You had something to prove." That pissed me off too. Was it my fault that these days ballet dancers and hairdressers are the studs and jocks are gay?

I was ahead of my time, that's all. So was Anudaba. When Anudaba was a kid he played with the girls and the other boys called him a sissy. He's still playing with the girls, only nobody thinks he's a sissy now except maybe Freeman Crocker, who I happen to think is queerer than a three-dollar bill, one of your British sergeant-major barracks faggots.

Our men's group went round and round with this sex role stuff; it's endless. Like one time we invited Phyllis Glass to our group. She's the Morristown lawyer who brought a discrimination suit when she was fired after having a sex-change operation. Her law firm said they didn't fire her at all; they'd hired a man, Phillip Glass, and since this person now insisted she was a woman, Phyllis Glass, she was not the person they'd hired.

Phyllis lost, but she was raising money for an appeal. She did guest spots on television talk shows, she made speeches. Sometimes, to look wholesome, she brought along her former wife and daughter. She and her wife still lived together, she said, "as woman and wife."

The night Phyllis Glass came to the men's group the doorbell rang and in walked this enormous person who filled our living room. She weighed two-fifty easy and had this big, deep voice and five o'clock shadow. Phyllis wore a dress, carried a pocketbook, and clambered about none too steadily on high heels. We could hear her coming up the stairs for ten minutes before she reached the fourth floor, out of breath.

Phyllis talked about what she called "gender discomfort." As she put it, "From birth, I was a female trapped in a male's body." She said there is no torture so excruciating as gender discomfort.

Phyllis really liked Anudaba. He treated her like a woman, opened the door for her, flirted with her. I suppose, as another kind of queer, I should have been especially sympathetic to Phyllis, but she gave me the creeps. I mean it's one thing to be attracted to the "wrong sex." Phyllis *was* the wrong sex.

This didn't bother Anudaba. For him the weirder, the better. I doubt Anudaba would talk to a person who wasn't weird in some way. If I was straight we'd never have become friends.

Weird people were always appearing at our men's group as guests. One spring night we had a Babadahs disciple in the Church Street apartment.

It was my doing. I'd been attending meditation meetings at the Babadahs Center in New York ever since I wandered in there one day. I was in Soho shopping. The Center is in this street of cast iron buildings filled with art galleries and import shops. Bright banners hang against the rust and soot. In the Center's window was a picture of this Indian with huge brown eyes. His eyes were so big they filled his face.

So this was Babadahs. I'd read about Babadahs. There'd been an article in the *Village Voice* which described wild orgies and freak-outs taking place at his New York center. "Why not?" I thought, going inside.

Only there weren't any wild orgies or freakouts. I was ushered into this incredibly comfortable, all-orange room where every-one sat on the floor, reverently looking at a blank television screen. Eerie music came on, the lights dimmed, and I dissolved into my surroundings.

The video was about the death in India of one of Babadahs' disciples, Swami Anand Gooba, a young Swiss guy of twenty-

three who had cancer. The footage was of him during the last
months of his life as he weakened and grew thinner. "I don't mind
dying in the least," Anand Gooba kept saying. "Dying is just what
I'm doing right now. Thank you, Babadahs."

Anand Gooba was shown dancing, attending darshan, eating in
the dining hall, where he waved his spoon wanly at the camera. He
was always surrounded by smiling disciples who kept hugging
him. It was like a big party.

Finally, Anand Gooba couldn't move about. Friends visited at
his bedside, bringing him little gifts. His parents flew in from
Switzerland.

In the last footage of Anand Gooba alive, his eyes were bright
and he smiled. His mother kissed him on the forehead. His father
stood calmly at the foot of the bed.

The whole ashram turned out for Anand Gooba's funeral. All
these orange people dancing and singing in Buddha Hall, celebrating. There was a stir, and four disciples carried in a litter with
Anand Gooba's body covered with flowers. Only the waxen face
and mala, which lay on top of the flowers, were visible.

The disciples gathered around the body, sprinkling rose petals.
Anand Gooba's parents smiled through their tears, swaying a little
to the music.

Then everything quieted down and Babadahs came in. He
strode to Anand Gooba's body and namasted. He namasted to
Anand Gooba's parents. He mounted the platform and namasted
to the disciples. They cheered him like he was running for office.
Then they quieted down again.

"Death," Babadahs said in this curious, high-pitched voice, "is
not death when one accepts it as part of life." He spoke with a lisp.
A speech defect, like Moses?

"Anand Gooba did not struggle against death," Babadahs continued. "He was in tune with the universe. He died enlightened. If
one dies enlightened, death is a beautiful thing." The video picture
switched back and forth between Babadahs and Anand Gooba.

"Anand Gooba's body was no good to him anymore, so he decided to leave it. We will all leave our present bodies some day, so
it is best to think of how we wish to leave them." Anand Gooba's
father was listening intently; his mother cried quietly.

"Anand Gooba died with great joy. There will be those who say,

'Ah, but if he died with joy, he must have been a perverted person, in love with death.' No, Anand Gooba died with joy because he was in love with life. When one is in love, one is not possessive. One can let go." Babadahs went on like this, speaking pure poetry. The expression in his saucer-sized eyes changed with every sentence. He looked like a wizard.

When Babadahs finished speaking he namasted and strode out of the hall. The litter with Anand Gooba was hoisted aloft and, with his parents and the disciples following—dancing and singing and clapping—it was carried throught he ashram to the banks of a small river, where it was placed on a bed of firewood.

As the flames rose the singing became louder. The final shot of the film was through the flames, on the other side of which Anand Gooba's parents knelt, half crying and half laughing, with disciples dancing around them, strewing clouds of rose petals in the air like confetti.

The lights came on in the screening room, where I had been reclining on an orange pillow. I was blown away; couldn't abide it that the video had ended, that I was back in my own world. "That was beautiful," I said to no one in particular.

When I got back to New Brunswick that night, Anudaba took one look at me and said, "What's up?"

"Nothing, nothing."

"Come on," he said. "What's with you?"

"Well," I said only half joking, "I just saw God."

Anudaba laughed. For him, religion in those days was a joke.

For me too. But I started going in to the Babadahs Center once a week on the bus. I asked Anudaba to go with me but he said, "You must be kidding." He did agree to my inviting a disciple to the men's group though. "Maybe I'll find out what's bugging you," he said.

The center in New York sent Ma Yoga Peedam, a graduate student at Columbia University. She came to New Jersey dressed in her orange outfit and mala. We lugged her equipment up to the fourth floor.

She put on a two-hour video of Babadahs talking called "The Sound of One Hand Clapping." That's all it was, Babadahs speaking to the camera. You'd think it would be boring.

But the man's face is so alive, so beautiful really, his leaps of expression, from joy to sorrow to humor, breathtaking. Sometimes his eyes nearly pop out of his head. He makes these stylized, lovely gestures, as if dancing with his skinny, brown hands.

No one in our raucous men's group stirred during those two hours. There's never been a church so quiet.

When the video ended, everyone had something to say except Anudaba. He just sat there, didn't say a word—which was unusual for him. He just stared at Ma Yoga Peedam. Did he have the hots for her or what?

After Ma Yoga Peedam and the men's group left, Anudaba remained sitting there, his expression blank. Then a look came onto his face that I had never seen before. It started at the back of his head and worked its way forward. I couldn't tell if he was going to laugh or cry or both. And then he did just that: he laughed and cried.

I don't mean he laughed and cried alternately. I mean he laughed and cried at the same time. Nonstop for fifteen minutes. I thought, Lord, he's flipping again.

"Love is its own reward," Anudaba said, repeating something Babadahs had said on the tape. He said it again: "Love is its own reward." He said it over and over. He wrote it down and put it on the bulletin board by the telephone. He opened the window of the apartment and shouted out into the night: "LOVE IS ITS OWN REWARD!"

"Asshole," someone in the darkness below called. But Anudaba just smiled. Then he said, "I'm going to India this summer, George. Want to come?"

Just like that. I'd been going in to the center in New York for months. He sees one tape and he's off to India. Doesn't need to come into New York to attend a meditation. Doesn't need to read any of the books. He's off to see Babadahs, and that's all there is to it.

I thought about going. I thought about it a lot. Here was my chance to be . . . well, special; to do something with my life besides what I'm supposed to do.

But my summer was planned: to finish as much of my second Swinburne book as possible so I could go for full professor in another year or so.

I'm always planning ahead. I get uptight when I haven't got

plans. I'm always making lists and crossing things off and making new lists. Going to India wasn't on my list.

Even if Babadahs were God I wouldn't just pick up and go to India. I'm not sure why, I just wouldn't. Maybe I've been around schools too long. If schools teach you anything, they teach you to not be all or nothing. They teach you to be cool.

So I stayed home that summer and worked on my book while Anudaba went to Boonam, gave up being Sidney Kantor, and became Swami Anudaba. I received a postcard from India signed with his new name. "Relax," he wrote. "Friends don't have to call me 'Swami.'"

When he came back in the fall, Anudaba had photographs of the ceremony in which he became a disciple. There was Babadahs placing the long mala around Anudaba's neck. There was Anudaba looking up at Babadahs with the same expression he'd had that night in the apartment after seeing the video. He looked like his face was going to bust.

In another photograph, Babadahs had his hand on Anudaba's head, his thumb digging into his forehead, pressing the third eye. There was such trust on Anudaba's face it was scary.

I envied him a little, but I pitied him too. With his orange clothes and mala he was a leper around the university now. Everybody in the English department laughed at him.

"Come off it, Sidney," they'd say, refusing to call him Anudaba. He walked down the hall in Hickman and people said, "There goes Agent Orange."

Freeman Crocker poked his head into Anudaba's office one day and sang, "Swami, how I love ya, how I love ya, my dear old Swami."

Anudaba just sat there.

So Freeman started in again, a real card. "Way down upon the Swami River . . . ."

It was awful. And there wasn't any way to fight it because professors are convinced they're the most open-minded, liberal people in the world. Sure they are! They're open-minded and liberal about what they're open-minded and liberal about. A freaky new religion isn't one of those things.

Religion's all right to study; we've got a religion department on campus. And it's all right to subscribe to some arteriosclerotic old religion as long as you don't take it too seriously. But suddenly getting religion? Coming down from the mountain with the word? All anyone could think of when they looked at Anudaba was the Moonies. Even the more charitable colleagues shook their heads and whispered "brainwashed."

Then Jonestown happened that November. Nine hundred followers of the Reverend Jim Jones drank cyanide in Guyana, and now people thought Anudaba wasn't just crazy; he was a menace. Next thing you knew he'd have students jumping off the Hickman Hall roof.

Even Carol Johnson turned on Anudaba when he went orange. Carol had been the only person in the department besides me who supported Anudaba whenever he got into trouble. When he went nuts that time she said, "Brilliant people are under pressure."

Carol and me and Anudaba were like the Three Musketeers in the department: the outsiders. Often she went with me to Tuesday Night Fix, was a real fan. But when Anudaba turned orange, she closed like a trap.

Carol and Anudaba had team-taught together, courses like "Sex Roles in American Literature," "Gender and Gynecology in Three American Poets: Bradstreet, Dickinson, and Rich." Carol always said Anudaba was the only male professor in the university she could team-teach with.

I thought Carol had the hots for Anudaba. She'd try to find out personal things about him from me. I didn't mind, except sometimes I'd think, I'm no pimp, why doesn't she ask him?

Carol talked to me a lot. She was a bit of a fag hag; I guess she thought I was safe.

She'd tell me all the gory details of her marriage to Felix, the Wall Street stockbroker she called "the straight-ahead pounder." "Felix's idea of lovemaking," Carol would say, "is to come running across the room and jump on you."

I think Carol fantasized that Anudaba was going to rescue her from Felix one day—Anudaba or somebody like him. She just couldn't make up her mind whether she wanted to be married to a guy who put on coat and tie to get the newspaper or one with earrings and a tattooed asshole.

I don't think Carol and Anudaba ever got it on, but sex was always crackling in the atmosphere, like a distant summer storm.

Everything they said was a double entendre.

Of course, Anudaba flirted with everyone. Carol? Maybe flirting with Anudaba was a way of toying with leaving Felix without having to do it. But when Anudaba returned from India orange, Carol took it personally. She thought he'd betrayed her somehow. "Sidney, a member of a cult?" she kept saying. "George, how could he do such a terrible thing?" You could almost hear her add "to me." Carol backed away from Anudaba as if from the plague. She stopped talking to him. She referred to Anudaba disgustedly as "him," curling her lip like he was a bug that had crawled out from under a rock. Now everything remotely related to Anudaba, any ideas they'd shared, were poison.

Carol stopped teaching feminist courses, went back to the safe, old Victorian poets she'd written her dissertation on. Her looks deteriorated. She never was any great beauty but now she started looking like a bag lady. She'd come to work in frowzy clothes and when there was a department party she'd hang on Felix's arm like she was welded to it.

Anudaba's becoming a disciple was no picnic for me either. I was living with someone with a weird name, who dressed in orange, who wore a long necklace with his guru's picture dangling from it. "Oh," people said to me, "you're the one who lives with the orange man."

Being Anudaba's roommate wasn't cool around the department either. Colleagues vied with each other taking pot shots at him; it was open-season on Anudaba. And, a little, on me.

I wish I could say I always stood up for him. Look, I called him "Anudaba," at least, I did that! That may not seem like any big deal, but everytime I said "Anudaba" eyebrows raised. It was like McCarthyism. You said "Anudaba" and that meant you were a pinko, nigger-loving, commie faggot. Since I already was one of those things, there was no point pushing my luck. One time in a Curriculum Committee meeting everyone kept referring to Anudaba as "Sidney" until I forgot myself and exploded, "His name is Anudaba, dammit."

You could have heard a pin drop. "You're not thinking of becoming an orange person too, are you George?" Carol Johnson asked, leading the charge. Freeman Crocker sat there next to her, smug as a turtle.

"Of course not," I said laughing. I'm real ashamed of that. Maybe it wasn't thirty pieces of silver, but it was ten or twelve. I *did* sometimes think of becoming a disciple. Besides, what business was it of hers?

After that meeting Carol took to calling me "Orangeade." Get it? Orange Aid. "Hey, Orangeade," she'd say, "How's your friend the swami?"

I just smiled and ignored it. Carol was real chummy with Freeman Crocker now—in fact, she made full professor that year. Anudaba was liable to go off to India some day for good, but I had to work with these people forever.

Sure I gave Anudaba support when we were alone, but I didn't want people in the English department identifying me with him too much. Besides, it wouldn't have been fair, dammit. I didn't go to India. I did what I was supposed to do: stayed home and busted my butt over Swinburne.

Okay, so I'm no hero. Maybe part of me was even glad Anudaba was under attack. Everyone asks today, "How could he quit his job? Leave his kids? Go to India?" But for me, inside somewhere, the question will always be, Why didn't I?

The attacks on Anudaba kept that miserable question from surfacing too often. They kept me from wondering whether I'll always be just ordinary—successful, but ordinary. I think that's what I most fear: being ordinary.

If Anudaba was aware of the uncertainty of my support he never said. Maybe he had gone so far out it didn't matter to him. The only thing he really thought about any more was India. He sat around all day and moped about India.

He was still popular with the students. The rest of us were so straight and here was this swami. The women students looked at his strange garb and said, "Isn't he cute?" Maybe they wondered what it would be like to get it on with a real, live, genuine swami.

But Anudaba was so preoccupied with India he wasn't much interested in women. He wasn't into teaching any more either. "I'm not sure I can keep getting up in front of these classes anymore, George," he'd say. "I don't know if I can keep playing these games."

He didn't do Tuesday Night Fix any more ("I've lost my calling," he halfheartedly joked). Also, our men's group was folding without his leadership, and the university fringe types were coming around less. It was as if Jesus had climbed down from the cross and said, "Forget it." It was real quiet in the apartment.

India, India, India. That's all he ever thought about, all he ever talked about. It could be a real bore.

To hear him tell it he had "glimpsed paradise" over there. If he had any balls, wouldn't he give up everything and go back there for good? But for what? he agonized. What was so great about losing your ego?

"What's happening over there is the most important thing on this planet," he screamed at me one night in the apartment.

"Okay," I shrugged. Why was he shouting at me? I hadn't said otherwise. This was his thing, not mine.

The next day Anudaba went to see Freeman Crocker and resigned effective the end of fall semester.

That night in the apartment we were both miserable. Anudaba because he'd done something irrevocable, probably a disaster. Me because I felt guilty; he'd wanted to talk the night before and I just wasn't there for him.

For a week we hardly communicated, couldn't find a way to break down the wall between us. I'd awaken to hear Anudaba walking around the apartment at night, not sleeping. During the day he looked terrible.

"Take it easy," I finally said to him one morning at breakfast as he sat there staring at his natural cereal. "I'm worried about you."

That broke the ice. He got up, put his head on my shoulder, wept.

The next day he went back to Freeman Crocker's office and tried to take back the resignation. Crocker did it, but he was going to get his pound of flesh. The paperwork was well-advanced, he wanted Anudaba to know.

"You have anything to say?" Crocker asked Anudaba in front of the whole department later that week. Crocker had just announced with grim satisfaction that Anudaba wasn't resigning after all. Not that he wanted Anudaba to stay; he just didn't want him thinking he had something better to do than be a professor.

Anudaba looked awful. He didn't so much apologize as recant. It was like a Moscow purge trial in that room.

Now, maybe because they sensed how fragile he was, smelled blood, everybody really got on Anudaba's case. "Why doesn't he quit jerking us around?" Carol Johnson said.

Sometimes I wonder whether Anudaba would have returned to India if our colleagues had been a little less unforgiving at this point. But they wanted him to grovel; they wanted his wings clipped good. No more hotshot campus celebrity. No more wild doings with the students. And while he was at it, couldn't he maybe give up this weird Indian cult? They were permitting him a wee little chance at rehabilitation, but it was going to be on their terms.

And let me be honest and not so holy: I didn't totally mind their terms; it wasn't doing *me* any good living with the department pariah—especially because the India issue wasn't resolved. In our apartment it was still on again/off again, day and night. I felt a little jerked around myself.

Then Anudaba received a letter from a friend in Boonam who told him Babadahs had mentioned him at a morning darshan. "Would you believe?" Anudaba said to me that night at dinner. "Here I am half a world away, going crazy, and He knows."

I said that maybe Babadahs mentioning him was a coincidence, but he didn't hear me. He carried the letter around in his pocket. He read it over and over.

Anudaba said he was going to see Freeman Crocker in the morning to resign again. "Hey," I said, "if you do it this time it's for real." I suggested he not resign, just take a leave of absence.

That's what he did. Took leave spring semester and went back to Boonam. "Let's hope he stays there." Freeman Crocker said.

I half felt the same way. I was sick and tired of carrying him on my back. Also, Anudaba had always been so impressive, so dazzling, you could hardly see me for the glare. Without him around, maybe I wouldn't have to play Sancho Panza to his Don Quixote, Doctor Watson to his Sherlock Holmes. I could do my own thing.

Anudaba wrote me regularly when he got back to India. Letters full of indecision. I didn't pay much attention because I was going through something of a crisis of my own. I had fallen head over heels in love.

I know this sounds corny, but I had never been in love before. Oh, I loved Sandy and the kids and my parents, but I'd never been *in* love before—the whole Hollywood, Doris Day, bells ringing, birds singing, heart-palpitating thing.

I think Babadahs had a lot to do with it—all his talk of surrendering the ego, letting go. But it was scary being in love. When I fell in love with Steven it was like falling off a cliff. That must be why we speak of *falling* in love. Falling in love is another way of heading for edge city.

I hardly knew Steven. And everything about us was different — on paper we're a disaster. I'm fifteen years older, eleven inches taller. I'm an agnostic Congregationalist from New England with mussed up hair and rumpled clothes; Steven is a heavy-duty Polack Catholic from Chicago, always has his shoes shined. He sells insurance, for crissake. I hate insurance men.

But when Steven and I met, it was instant chemistry. We just fit. I wanted to marry Steven. I wished I could have children with him, grandchildren. Someday I wanted us to be buried under the same tombstone. A week after we met, Steven moved into my apartment.

There was only one problem. Steven had a relationship with another guy, Richard, who was from out of town, married, had six kids. He came to New Jersey on business every Thursday, and Steven spent Thursday nights with him at his tiny apartment in Princeton. They'd been seeing each other for two years on a "same time next Thursday" basis.

Thursday nights were an agony for me. I stayed late at Rutgers or went to the movies. Several times I went back to cruising Seminary Place; I had to distract myself in some way. Aside from my misery, I didn't want to turn Steven off by becoming a nag. I'm not a drinker, but some Thursday nights I sat in the apartment and drank myself stupid.

I even had a one-night stand with a woman. Jean, her name was, an instructor in Art History. I met her at the dean's house at a party.

She was brand-new at the university, didn't know anyone. So we talked. I talked about Steven, but that didn't stop her from inviting me back to her place across the Raritan River in Highland Park. She had some great grass. Before I knew it, there I was in bed with a woman. "You're a wonderful lover," Jean said, "so considerate." That was nice to hear, but there's nothing like being with a woman, even stoned, to convince you you're gay.

While all this was going on, Anudaba kept writing and asking, What should I do? His deadline for informing the university about coming back fall semester was fast approaching. How the hell did

I know what he should do? I had enough problems of my own. Our problems got resolved at about the same time. Steven decided not to see Richard any more. Richard had met a yuppie businesswoman in Princeton and wanted to alternate seeing her and Steven Thursday nights. "I don't take it personally," Steven said, "but his having a wife and kids is one thing; having a girl friend is another. To hell with these bisexual jerks who want to have their cocks and eat them too."

Steven and I celebrated at J. August's restaurant, and the next day we bought this wine red brocade Empire sofa we had been craving in Aardvark's Antiques on French Street.

A week later I received a letter from Anudaba saying he had decided to remain in India. Selfishly, I was glad. I didn't have room for him in my life—literally didn't have room with Steven living with me.

Also, things were so much better for me in the department with Anudaba gone for good. A lot of his old students gravitated toward me. And now that I was out from under his cloud, Freeman Crocker was a lot friendlier. He began hinting that I might be put up for promotion in another year or so.

Anudaba enclosed a resignation letter for Crocker. It was written in orange felt tip. "Dear Freeman," it said.

Only I am more relieved than you that I hereby resign my position with Rutgers effective immediately. I am sorry for any difficulties caused the department by my uncertain status over the past months. If you or any of my former colleagues pass through India at any time I should be only too happy to show you the sights.

With the blessings of Babadahs, I remain,

Yours sincerely,

Swami Anudaba

P.S. Since this is my official resignation from the university, I had better sign also with my old name to make it legal. Here goes.

Sidney Kantor

Anudaba didn't say in his letter to me what had finally gotten him to resign. But he did mention "this beautiful Belgian Ma I've met here. You should see her George." To make sure I saw her, he'd enclosed a photograph of the two of them nude. They were looking at the camera with impish smiles on their faces and Anudaba was giving the camera the finger. On the back of the photograph the woman had written, "George, Anudaba has told me so much about you, I have the hots for you too. Love, Ma Prem Isabel."

Ma Prem Isabel was a terrific-looking woman. She was slim but statuesque, with marvelous breasts. Her eyes were violently green and looked into the camera with humor and insolence. I imagined her saying "the hots" with her Belgian accent: "ze huts."

After this, I didn't hear from Anudaba so often. Maybe it was because he was content. *I* was certainly content. Oh, I occasionally lusted after a cute guy, but I felt more committed to Steven than to anyone or anything before in my life.

This domestic bliss was great for my career. My second book on Swinburne came out and got terrific reviews. The *New York Times* said, "This is the definitive Swinburne. It will be a long time before Smith's effort is bested."

I took Steven with me to the reception put on by the publisher, which was like a big coming-out party for us. I also took him up to New Hampshire to meet my mother. Everything went amazingly smoothly after the initial awkwardness. My mother said, "At least you gave me grandchildren first."

Things went great between my kids and Steven too. The kids visited regularly and got used to us pretty quickly. Kids never think of their parents as sexual anyway, so it wasn't necessary for me to say, "Hey, this is who I do it with."

It was a little difficult with Sandy—nothing major. She said, "Learning you're gay was one thing; meeting your lover is another." She kept walking around Steven, eyeing him for some clues to his nature.

"Look," I told her, "it isn't so easy seeing you with another man either." This was at a party at Elaine's house where Sandy had come with her boyfriend, a nice guy actually.

Elaine invites me out to Griggstown regularly these days, though I don't go too often. It's not me that Elaine's inviting but Anudaba's ghost. She's hoping to experience him through me or at least get some news.

Everyone Elaine invites to these parties was a friend of hers and Anudaba's. I'm never sure whether I'm at a party or a reunion. It's "Waiting for Godot" and, as usual, Godot isn't coming. At Elaine's parties you can feel Anudaba all around you. When you talk to Elaine she always looks over your shoulder, as if she's watching for him.

I'd gone this time because I knew Sandy and my kids would be there and also because I wanted to introduce Steven around. And it was an okay party—maybe because we were outside, where I could more easily keep Elaine from cornering me. Friends of Elaine's had a little flute and violin combo, and their madrigals filled the night air. Paperbag lanterns were lit all the way down to the Millstone River, and everyone strolled down there and watched the fish jump.

I was standing by the river when Elaine softly approached and said she wanted to talk to me. "Alone," she said. I excused myself from Steven—felt bad leaving him; he didn't know anyone there—and went back to the house with her and into the study.

It was strange being with her in the room where Anudaba had once spent so much of his time. There were reminders of him everywhere, from the rack of pipes he stopped smoking years ago to all that American literature covering the walls, first editions and old bindings mixed in with the paperbacks. On the fireplace mantel were photographs of Anudaba's European ancestors: women in kerchiefs, men with beards and skullcaps.

I used to like being in this room with Anudaba. It was an aesthetic respite from my split-level box next door and from Hickman Hall's glassy ugliness. I wondered if Elaine had consciously chosen this room for our talk.

"I hear he's going to stay there," Elaine said with no preliminaries.

"Yes," I replied. Whenever I was with Elaine I said as little as possible. She was always pumping me for information about Anudaba. I was never sure whether something I said might get him in trouble.

"Did you know Jane is over there now?"

I hadn't known that, but I wasn't totally surprised. I'd seen Jane once at the Babadahs Center in New York, where I still went sometimes. They were having a Dynamic Meditation that night. I waved to her across the room as we jumped up and down, and she blushed. Afterwards I looked for her, but she was gone.

Jane was awkward and shy, had always had a lousy image of herself. And it didn't help when, a few months before, she'd been raped — if that's what it was — by two drunken men in their twenties.

Jane had been hitchhiking back to Griggstown from New Brunswick and they'd picked her up and rode around with her, alternately having sex with her in the back seat before depositing her, finally, in front of her house. Jane hadn't resisted. It was as if she had so little sense of herself she wasn't capable of resisting anyone about anything.

Elaine hadn't found out about it until a month later when Jane mentioned it casually. When Elaine asked her why she hadn't said anything, Jane shrugged, "Well, it wasn't any big deal."

Elaine had made a point of dropping by my office in Hickman Hall to tell me about it. "It wouldn't have happened if Sidney was a responsible father," she said. I didn't know about that. It might have had more to do with Elaine's spinelessness than Anudaba's absence.

Every conversation I have with Elaine is another battle in her continuing war with Anudaba — a war he long ago quit. I'm supposed to witness these battles, record them. Elaine steers our conversation around to where I can either say nothing and accept what she's left hanging in the air — usually a not-so-veiled condemnation of Anudaba as a father — or get into an argument with her. Aside from the unpleasantness of any argument, with Elaine there's no point. She never stands and fights. She manages to both retreat *and* keep her moral superiority intact.

Lord knows my feelings about Anudaba aren't unmixed. There are things I love about him, things I don't. I could sympathize with Elaine if she ever gave me the chance. She sees herself as Anudaba's victim. Okay, I've felt that way myself sometimes.

Well, maybe not his victim. He's just stronger than I am. Stronger than Elaine and stronger than me. Under certain circumstances Elaine and I might have made common cause. In fact, more than once I've looked at Elaine and thought, You know, she's kind of pretty.

But every time I talk with Elaine my sympathy for her evaporates. She always lays trips, makes me feel used. Like now she said, "You don't think Jane will become a disciple, do you, George?" Only it sounded like she wanted to know what *I* was doing to make sure Jane didn't become a disciple.

The truth is, becoming a disciple might be good for Jane. Life wasn't too promising for her in New Jersey. The ashram could shape her up.

Her father's a disciple. What's so bad about following in your father's footsteps? Maybe it's like joining the family business.

Besides, Elaine couldn't rightly bitch about Jane being with Anudaba in India *and* bitch about him abandoning his kids.

Harry, Anudaba's son, seemed to be doing fine without him in the States. "Heck," Harry told me earlier at the party, "I'm never home anyway." He thought it "funny" his father had become "some kind of Indian weirdo." Other kids' fathers were corporate lawyers or shoelace manufacturers. "I tell them my father is a swami. Blows them away."

Harry seemed almost enthusiastic about his father being in India. "Dad's doing his thing," Harry said, "and I'm doing mine. It isn't as if I'm an orphan or anything."

Harry's a senior in high school and a whiz with computers. In *Time* magazine's cover story on computers, Harry and some other kids appeared in a picture with the caption, "Outstripping their elders."

Not bad: *Time* magazine. I've never appeared in *Time* magazine.

Still, Elaine worries about Harry. That's Elaine's thing: worrying. She acts like she's got a monopoly, like she's cornered the market on worrying.

Harry's off to college in another year, which couldn't be too soon to get out of Elaine's orbit. Meanwhile, he's a bit of a problem. Cracked up the family Volvo a while back riding around the Millstone Valley with friends, and he and Elaine fight day and night. Elaine always says, "You'll see things differently when you're a little older, Harry," which, of course, really revs Harry's motors.

Harry came in while I was talking with Elaine in the study. "For crissake, Mom," he demanded, "where's the rest of the wine?"

His interruption provided my excuse to escape. "You *will* let me know if you hear anything about Jane?" Elaine called after me, her voice full of restrained anger at Harry for barging in just when she thought she was getting somewhere with me.

"Of course," I said, walking out into the night and taking the first real breath in fifteen minutes. I could hear Harry's high-pitched anger and Elaine's too soft response, and I remembered something Anudaba had said before going to India for good: "I can do more for the kids away from Elaine, even in India, than I ever could in Griggstown."

A few weeks later I got a letter from Anudaba in which he said Jane had become a disciple. Her name was now Ma Prem Jane. "Not fair," he wrote, "me with this weird name, she still 'Jane.'" Also, they're training her to be the ashram personnel chief while her poor old dad goes on doing K.P. Frosts my ass." But I could tell he was proud.

Anudaba's letter put me in a spot. I'd promised to tell Elaine if I heard anything about Jane, but I didn't want to talk to Elaine—especially not about this. Talking with Elaine is like walking through a swamp. You never know when you're going to get sucked in. Luckily, I ran into Anudaba's mother, Mildred Kantor, just outside Grand Central Station in New York City, and she invited me to tea.

I knew Mrs. Kantor from seeing her at the house in Griggstown. That's some lady. Almost seventy years old and she goes all the way to India to visit Anudaba. But I could see where she might be less easy to take if she were your mother.

"So, George," she said when we were seated in Schraft's, "What do you think of all this?"

Before I could ask what "this" referred to, she said: "I'll tell you what *I* think about it. I think it's a disgrace."

I nodded noncommittally.

"With all the troubles in the world—hunger, pollution, terrorists . . . to waste his life on this Indian monkey business. And now Jane, too."

"Maybe Babadahs is a way of leapfrogging over those problems," I ventured. "Can't get up the staircase, you take the fire escape."

"Let me ask you something, George," she said. I wasn't sure if she'd heard me or not. "You're a homo, right?"

"Yes," I said, wondering what that had to do with it.

"So, tell me: here you are, a perfectly nice and normal-looking man. You were married, you have children. And Sidney: only a few years ago, a professor like you, a nice home and family. What is going on, can you tell me that, George? Is the world becoming crazy or is it becoming crazy?"

"The world's always been 'crazy,'" I replied. "Babadahs says—"

"Babadahs, Shmabadahs! You should excuse me, George, but I *know* what Babadahs says; I was there. Every lunatic has a few good things to say. Even Hitler—"

"You equate Babadahs with Hitler?" What could I say to that? When it comes to Hitler, Jews ought to know. Still, I thought I had enough credentials to press on. "Hitler was a mass murderer. Babadahs preaches love."

"Love?" she said. "Love is giving up your traditions, your family?"

"Babadahs says those things enslave us. He says we have to rid ourselves of all that baggage."

"That baggage," Mildred Kantor said, "that baggage, George, is who we are."

It was a stalemate and there was no point going on. But the tea was a success for me nevertheless. Mrs. Kantor was going to Griggstown that weekend and would carry the message about Jane to Elaine. Anything was worth not having to talk to Elaine.

Still, it was with some interest that I awaited Elaine in my office earlier today. She'd called to say she had some very particular things to tell me.

Some months had gone by since her party and since I had tea with Mrs. Kantor in New York. Anudaba had finally been relieved of K.P. duties and was editing a gorgeous ashram magazine called *Babadahs*. "They decided I'd dropped sufficient ego," he'd penned on the cover of the first issue when he sent it to me.

The magazine went to all disciples worldwide, had almost half a million circulation. "This isn't some dumb scholarly journal nobody reads," Anudaba wrote. "This is big time, George."

I chanced passing the magazine around in the English department. Surprise: everybody was delighted. Okay, so the guy's a nut. But he hasn't resigned from the academic fraternity altogether; he's still publishing.

I continued to keep Anudaba's letters to myself. He'd write things like, "I'm working on getting beyond jealousy, George.

Isabel has. She watches me having sex with someone else and rubs my back."

Anudaba wrote that the ashram's sexual ways were making trouble in India. The see-through robes and hugging in the streets made the righteous Hindus gape in disbelief. Children threw rocks. A blonde disciple from Sweden was attacked by a gang in an alley.

Sex wasn't the only reason the ashram was in trouble. In India you do poverty and humility for ten years before a Master will even take you on, and you'll be a disciple another ten years before you're called Swami. Babadahs puts the mala on you right off and—Shazzam! you're a Swami.

This drives the Hindus crazy. One night an ashram dormitory was firebombed. "They just threw a Molotov cocktail over the wall," Anudaba wrote. He said the ashram was thinking of moving to a place where they wouldn't have to worry so much about security. At the time I paid little attention.

Babadahs was getting a hard time outside India too. A movie was being shown in avant garde movie houses called *Ashram: The Story of the Sex Guru*. I went into the city to see it at the Art Cinema in Greenwich Village, hoping to catch a glimpse of Anudaba if nothing else. That's what I caught: a glimpse. There he was, hugging somebody. At least I think it was him.

There wasn't any sex in the movie at all. In one scene of a nude encounter group, disciples hit each other with foam rubber bats. If there was sex in the movie, that was it. But still, when I came out of the theatre, a long line of people was waiting to get in, everybody nervous and dry-mouthed in anticipation.

Life magazine had a story about movie star and millionaire disciples called "Sex Guru Gains Prominent Adherents." There it was again: "sex guru." What was this sex guru shit? *Life* had photographs from what looked like the same nude encounter group as in the movie.

Everywhere I turned there was news of Babadahs. The *New York Times* ran a story about a disciple in the United States Air Force, in trouble for openly displaying his mala. The Air Force first said he couldn't wear it. Then they said he could wear it if it was covered up, inside his shirt, like a cross or Star of David. The disciple said "Nuts." There was a picture of him saluting in his blue dress uniform, all hundred and eight wooden beads of the mala around his neck and Babadahs staring out from among the brass buttons on his chest.

Babadahs was everywhere these days. You couldn't walk into a bookstore without seeing his face on half the books in the religion and philosophy sections. You couldn't find Kahlil Gibran on those shelves anymore; just Babadahs.

And you'd see disciples everywhere. My son and I were in Yankee Stadium, and two rows in front of us was a disciple with *his* son. The kid had Oshkosh B'Gosh overalls dyed orange and a cute, miniature mala around his neck.

It gave me a twinge. I mean, that could have been Ralph and me.

I jumped into a cab at Penn Station in New York in a torrential rainstorm only to discover that my driver was dressed in orange. "You're not . . . ." He waved his mala at me over his shoulder. Everyone was becoming orange except me.

You even started to see articles on Babadahs in local newspapers. The *New Brunswick Home News* had one. It was the usual "sex guru" stuff, but I loved the title: "Painting the World Orange."

I was reading that article when I heard Elaine get off the elevator. I knew it was Elaine by the way she walked down the hall towards my office — tentatively, as if each step were a challenge. I quickly folded the newspaper and slipped it into my desk drawer. No sense waving a flag in front of her.

Elaine took her own sweet time getting around to the purpose of her visit. She relished having information I didn't have, was going to savor it as long as possible. We talked about Sandy, about Griggstown, about a graduate course in English Elaine is taking at Rutgers. Why does Elaine have to study here? I swear: she knows what's going on in the English department better than I do.

Finally, Elaine got down to business. She'd received a letter from Jane. In it were three items of news she wanted to share with me.

I was pissed that I was getting this from Elaine instead of from Anudaba, but I sat still and listened.

Anudaba had gotten married — "to a Ma Prem Isabel," Elaine said. She passed this on to me as an amusing curiosity. "It couldn't be very good for Sidney," she said, as if speaking disinterestedly about a flaky brother. "He *so* wanted to be free."

The second item of news was that the ashram at Boonam was being disbanded. There had been more attacks in the streets, another firebombing. An Indian politician had been railing against Babadahs in the Parliament.

There's some background on Elaine's third piece of information which, for me, was a mindblower. Anudaba and I had been writing back and forth about Steven and me visiting the ashram this coming summer, after the academic year ends. We were planning an Asian trip — including Singapore, Thailand, and Japan; we love oriental food — with a stopover in India.

I was keen on Steven and Anudaba meeting each other. I was also keen on seeing Anudaba myself. It was a year and a half already.

Finally, I was excited about attending Babadahs' darshans — a little scared too. I mean, what if I flipped out over him? What if I didn't?

Either way, maybe it would be all right. I'd always felt bad about not going to India with Anudaba two summers ago. Now, even if just as a tourist, I was going.

But in his last letter Anudaba had said, "Hold everything, George; things are up in the air here. I'll get back to you." This was irritating. What was going on?

So I was uptight, with no word from Anudaba as to whether Steven and I should complete our travel plans for the summer — and the travel sgency, which was holding our deposit, calling me daily asking, "Yes or no?" — when Elaine breathlessly dropped the last piece of information on me.

"They're coming to the United States," she said. "Sidney, Jane, Babadahs, everybody. There's talk of setting up the ashram here in America."

III

A BLISS CASE

For I have come to set a man against his father
and a daughter against her mother, and a daughter-
in-law against her mother-in-law; and a man's foes
will be those of his household.

Jesus
Matthew 10:34-36

September 1983

ALL I EVER WANTED was for him to love me. But he was too busy loving everyone and everything else. "Look," he'd say. "Look at this flower. Look at these grains of pollen. Look how beautiful it all is. Don't you just love it?"

He loved flowers and he loved people and he loved God. He just didn't love me.

I was in love with him. To my shame, I probably still am. But why couldn't he see that I was a flower too? I needed watering and I needed sunlight, and I needed admiration, and he never gave me any of those things. So I withered. I've been withering now for as long as I can remember.

He's a beautiful man—outside, anyway. Look at those eyes. He looks just like Jesus. Sometimes I thought he *was* Jesus: that *I* had married Jesus. What more romantic fate for a Methodist girl from Nebraska than to marry a New York Jew who, it turns out, is Jesus?

I was his wife, but I was never his partner. He was always three steps ahead of me. As soon as I caught on to what he was doing he was doing something else. I even tried smoking marijuana so as to be with him. But by the time I smoked marijuana he didn't anymore.

Years before he had said, "There are two kinds of people, Elaine: those who smoke dope and those who don't," and it was clear with which group he thought virtue resided.

By the time I tried it, marijuana smokers were moving on to either cocaine or God. And Sidney was nothing if he wasn't trendy. "I don't need dope to get high anymore," he said.

When I smoked marijuana that one time I was proud of myself; I went totally out of control. I started singing and dancing around the living room. I tried to get Sidney to make love to me, but he looked at me in disgust. Sidney said marijuana was now "counter-revolutionary." Apparently, once the hated middle class does something, it is counterrevolutionary. And I am nothing if not middle class.

At least, that is what Sidney always told me. "You're so disgustingly middle class." Oh, I was middle class all right. He'd come home from Rutgers an hour or two after he said he would—*if* he said he would be home by a certain time and *if* he came home—and

I'd have the table set with linen and china and I'd have been working all day to make a gourmet meal.

Sidney would eat in five minutes and go into the living room to
listen to the Rolling Stones and smoke marijuana with the children
while I did the dishes. I didn't want the children smoking; I'd talk
to Sidney about it. But as they lay on the rug and smoked, and I
stood at the kitchen sink, my hands turning red in the dishwater,
I'd hear Sidney say to the children, "Mother's so middle class."

Look, I just wanted to be with him, to share with him, to do what
he was doing. I'd have been his willing acolyte in any cause he cared
to name. When he stopped smoking marijuana and began sitting
around in a trance I'd say, "Can't we be mystical together? Isn't that
what marriage ought to be, a mystical union?"

When Sidney replied, if he replied, he'd say, "It's impossible to be
mystical together, Elaine. But nobody's stopping you from being
mystical one your own." When Sidney got enthusiastic about
something it became his private property.

The irony is that I was into spiritual things before he was — and I
don't just mean the church. I only turned to the church out of
desperation. Before that, I did Yoga. I did Transcendental Meditation. Sidney found it convenient to forget that it was I who intro-
duced him to the writings of Baba Ram Dass. Sidney found it
convenient to forget a lot of things.

But there was space for only one of us to be the mystic and Sidney
squatted squarely in the center of it. Somebody had to keep the
house clean.

So he meditated and I vacuumed. He carried on about the beauty
of flowers; I grew the flowers. I don't mean he never helped me.
Every once in a while he came on like a feminist guerilla, demanding he be allowed to martyr himself washing the ring off the bath-
tub. How he carried on. The children and I had to leave the house
so he could concentrate.

It wasn't worth the stress. And besides, it didn't matter to me that
much whether he helped around the house or not. All I really
wanted from him was a kind word. I'd keep knocking on the door
of his soul saying, "Let me in for Christ's sake," but one thing I was
fast learning about saints is that they don't share.

And Sidney was a kind of saint. He had that glow and those eyes
and everyone thought he was going to take over the world some-

day. He was Svengali and Rasputin and Jesus and Moses and Mohammed and Napoleon all wrapped up in one. The students worshipped him.

I remember Sidney's Twentieth Century Lit class sitting around
on the grass in our backyard, the students looking up at him in
wonder. Sidney read Allen Ginsberg aloud; the students smiled on
cue.

A joint was being passed around. This was when Sidney was
smoking marijuana all the time. He kept a bong by our bedside and
lit it when he got up in the morning. He prepared his lectures while
high. His syllabi read like stream of consciousness. "This isn't a
syllabus, it's a word painting," Sidney said as he distributed it to his
students.

He worried me. He had been a fine critic but now that wasn't
enough for him. "I don't want to write about Walt Whitman," he
would say. "I want to *be* Whitman." I wasn't sure by what alchemy
he expected to become Whitman; he never wrote now.

Sidney turned everything into a Happening. Not just at the university but at home too. Shopping at the A & P, playing with the
children, everything. Even our lovemaking. One time he rigged
up a rope in our bedroom and wanted me to swing on it naked.

The house became a psychedelic theatre. Sidney wired the rafters with microphones, speakers and lights, and painted the classic
dentils of the living room cornice chartreuse. "Enough of this col-
onial shit," he said.

Everyone in the family had to get into the spirit of the Happenings. "A family is a floating crap game," Sidney liked to say. He
organized role-playing sessions in which the children got to play
each other or us. "Okay, Harry," he would say, "you be me today;
I'll be you." All day long Sidney and Harry stomped around the
house in each other's clothes.

Evenings and weekends were perpetual psychodrama. It was
impossible to impose any kind of discipline. Meals were not to take
place at a particular time but "when the vibes were right." There
was to be no bedtime for the children. "Don't you think kids are
smart enough to know when they're sleepy?" he would say. When
I wouldn't go along with the plan Sidney called me a "domestic
fascist." He said domestic fascists were the worst kind.

Despite his democratic pretensions, Sidney insisted we take the children out of the public schools. "I don't want them to be like everyone else," he would say. Sidney had a horror of our children being taken for living in the suburbs.

"But they *do* live in the suburbs," I would say.

"That's okay," Sidney said. "They still don't have to be burbettes."

The kids went to a place called Freedom School which a lady named Mimi Fontaine ran in her barn just outside of Millstone, the next town up along the canal. All ages of children were mixed in together. Mimi was Secretary-Treasurer of the National Association for Children's Rights. She used to say, "Blacks, women, gays, and old people aren't oppressed; children are oppressed." Mimi thought it was outrageous that men and women can get divorced but children are "stuck with the family they were born into."

The Freedom School kids went off on day-long field trips to museums, to Broadway matinees, to hunt Indian arrowheads and dinosaur bones, to march in peace parades. They visited the offices of Chinese acupuncturists. Every morning when they got to school, instead of pledging allegiance to the flag, they did yoga.

Out behind the barn was a garden where each child had his own plot and grew vegetables. In the winter they worked on their compost piles. I had to send along egg shells and orange peels and coffee grounds with the children every day, wrapped carefully so as not to be confused with their lunch.

The children had an orchestra for which they made their own musical instruments — guitars out of cigar boxes and rubberbands, xylophones out of glasses filled with different levels of water which they rapped with pencils.

They also had pets at the school. Hamsters, gerbils, guinea pigs. A big old sleepy turtle. A garter snake.

It was all terribly creative, only my children never got any reading, writing, or arithmetic in that school. To this day they can't spell.

A basic difference between Sidney and me is that I'd have been happy enough for the children to be ordinary, normal. Sidney wanted them to save the world. "The trouble with you, Elaine," Sidney said, "is you can't see beyond the picket fence." Maybe so. My vision of the future was Sidney and me *behind* that picket fence in rocking chairs on the porch, the kids coming to visit with our grandchildren. "You want me to barf?" Sidney said.

Sidney was so terribly *with it*. His favorite expression was, "I hear ya." He returned with it from a trip to California. When the children demanded something, when I made a complaint, Sidney said, "I hear ya." He never did anything about it; he just said, "I hear ya." Sometimes when he said "I hear ya" I thought I would run screaming out into the night. The children parroted Sidney. "I hear ya," little Jane would say, not knowing what it signified.

Our house became the gathering place for every unusual person in the Millstone Valley. At all hours of day or night people could be found somewhere in our house "rapping" as Sidney liked to call it. Some of these people practically lived in our house. I'd say to Sidney, "Why can't we have anyone over who is normal?"

It was as if the Millstone River and Delaware and Raritan Canal were carrying some common freight of looniness through the valley and it was all lapping up on our shore. One of Sidney's friends, crazy on L.S.D., came over to our house determined to rid us forever of dandelions. I heard explosions in the front yard and rushed out to discover this young man taking aim at a dandelion clump with a .22 rifle. Sometimes I wonder whether George Smith would have decided he was homosexual if he hadn't lived in the valley.

In the valley everyone wanders in and out of everyone else's house. Once I got up in the middle of the night sensing something was wrong. I nudged Sidney, but he was dead to the world. There was a flickering light on the wall outside our bedroom and a humming sound coming from downstairs. Thinking the house was on fire I charged down the staircase in my nightgown to discover a huge man I had never seen before seated in the living room before a mandala lamp, incense sticks smoking in my Swedish ivy. It must have been three in the morning, and this behemoth in a flannel shirt and dark glasses sat there chanting in Hindi. I screamed.

"Who the hell are *you?*" this man wanted to know.

When I crept back upstairs, Sidney said, "Will you quit making such a racket? That's just Leroy."

Again, maybe it's the river and canal influence. Who can get fixated on private property with all that water sweeping by, regularly changing boundary lines? The rest of central Jersey is asphalt, so when it rains, the water runs down into our valley. When there's a hurricane the valley becomes a sheet of water, moving like the Mississippi through the flatlands. There's no way to get out; all the roads are covered. Everyone becomes terribly nice to everyone else because of the natural disaster.

Our house is built just on the edge of the flood plain and we've had storms where the water crept up to our back door. One time it poured in over the sill. "Quick," I yelled to the children. We moved all the books and furniture upstairs. We couldn't move the piano. The water came into the kitchen and then into the living room, where it lapped around the piano legs.

The basement filled with water altogether. It reached five feet down there. There's still a mark on the wall.

Sidney's wine racks disintegrated and the bottles got loose and started smacking up against the wall. Sidney never liked me to phone him at the university, but this time I did. No luck. He was probably off screwing some student. Then he came home furious that his wine cellar was demolished. "Why didn't you call me?" he said.

Sidney was particularly upset by all the damage because one of his classes was supposed to meet at our house a few days later. Sidney's classes fit right in at our house, especially as they weren't classes in the conventional sense. I remember one time Sidney blindfolded everyone in the Modern Poetry class. The students had to really touch another person's hand, really touch another person's face. What all this touching had to do with literature was beyond me.

But the students liked it well enough. Sidney was a relief from their other classes, where professors delivered the same lectures year after year, reading from stacks of yellowing notecards held together by thick rubber bands. All that ever changed about those notes is sometimes the rubber bands dried out and had to be replaced.

I often wonder why Sidney quit the university. He loved to teach. He says he quit to become a Babadahs disciple, but I think it had more to do with the students changing. Sidney had been just like the students. They smoked marijuana, Sidney smoked marijuana. They wore jeans with patches, he wore jeans with patches. They grew their hair long, he grew his hair long.

By the late seventies, Sidney's style contrasted sharply with the students' preppie clothes and short hair. These students had their own credit cards; all they wanted out of the university were jobs as accountants. Sidney's classes were still heavily enrolled, but students would say to one another, "That Professor Kantor, he's a character."

Back in the late sixties and early seventies Sidney walked on water as far as the students were concerned. The young men in his classes affected his soulful look. The young women jiggled about without bras to attract his attention.

The students followed Sidney like he was the Pied Piper of Hamelin. Later, I learned, some of them followed him right into his bed.

One of these students came to see me. The phone rings and a voice asks, "Is this Mrs. Kantor?"

"Yes," I say.

"Mrs. Kantor, this is Ling Po. I guess you know who I am."

"No," I say, "I don't know who you are."

Ling Po is this beautiful Eurasian who has been having an affair with Sidney. Now he's told her it's over. She wants my advice.

Get in line, I want to tell her, I was here first. Sidney didn't love me long before he didn't love you.

This took place when Sidney was already spending most of his time at George Smith's New Brunswick apartment. Ah, that George. He's another story.

Anyway, Ling Po, an English major who has been starring in Sidney's campus Happenings, has also been starring in his bed. She says, "Maybe you won't mind talking with me about my situation, since Sidney left you a long time ago." I didn't tell her that this was the first I knew Sidney *had* left me.

"I love him so much," she tells me when she arrives in Griggstown in a beat-up VW bug. "What am I going to do?"

So I made tea for Ling Po and we sat around and talked about her "situation." Maybe I did some good. The day before she had tried to hang herself. She had gotten a noose of clothesline ready in her closet and stood on a chair and put the noose around her neck. "But then I had this terrible itch. My knee itched. So I took off the noose to scratch my knee, and, while leaning over, I fell off the chair and hit my head and then killing myself seemed like a dumb idea."

Ling Po told me, "I didn't believe it was possible Sidney could

look at me like that without it being forever. I should have known
better: all the girls put on makeup to go to his classes. He looks at
everyone that way."

I knew that look. I had experienced its full intensity years ago
and faint glimpses of it over the years since. Those faint glimpses
which somehow kept me going, thinking, He'll love me soon. I
just know it.

And he did love me. Probably still does. He just doesn't love me
any more than he loves Ling Po or a thousand other women. He's
incapable of loving a woman. He loves *women*. Like he loves flowers. Like he loves God. What women have always been attracted to
in Sidney, like moths to a flame, was, they suspected (but could
never admit to themselves), that quality in him of being just out of
reach.

Ling Po would have followed Sidney to the ends of the earth. *I*
would have followed Sidney to the ends of the earth. But Sidney
traveled light.

That's what's so strange about this Babadahs business. Sidney
used to *be* Babadahs. He had half of New Brunswick and Griggstown bowing down at his feet. So what does he do? He goes off
to India and prostrates himself at someone else's feet.

Looking back I know why I could never have satisfied him.
Neither me nor any of the other women who worshipped him. He
liked being worshipped — but just so far. He could never respect
anyone who worshipped him. Deep inside *he* wanted to be the
worshipper.

Sidney wanted to surrender. And here in New Jersey, where he
was God, he couldn't do that. So he went off to India and fell at
God's feet. Babadahs really had Sidney's number when he named
him Anudaba, Slave of Slaves.

But this is Sidney. What about me? How did I ever get involved
with such a person, have two children with him, allow myself to be
his perpetual victim? What is the matter with me? He may be a
louse, but why am I so craven?

Do you believe that I actually had Sidney and his new wife Ma
Prem Isabel over to lunch? This man destroys me and I invite him
to lunch with his new wife.

Well, it could have been worse. I might have said yes when he
asked if they could live here.

He actually asked. I knew the ashram had disbanded and Baba-dahs was somewhere in America getting treatment for his aller-gies; Jane was already back from India staying with me. But it was still a shock when I got Sidney's phone call from Kennedy Airport at five in the morning.

"Elaine," the voice said, as I struggled up out of sleep. "This is Anudaba."

"Who?" I said.

"Anudaba. Sidney." I remember thinking he must want something or he wouldn't use his old name. Many's the time I had been corrected for using it. "We've just flown in from India. Can we stay with you in Griggstown?"

Sidney figured if Jane was staying with me, why not him? And, if him, why not his new wife, Ma Prem Isabel? Arriving from India penniless and with parasites, he thinks, Why not stay at the old homestead? There's only the inconvenience of an ex-wife living there. His voice suggested that if I were any kind of human being I wouldn't stand on ceremony.

I don't know whether I was madder at him for asking or at myself for saying no, but thank God I said no. Even I have limits to my abjectness. "Absolutely not," I said.

"Okay," Sidney said, trying to sound as cool and unconcerned as possible while letting the guilt hang in the air. "Don't get uptight."

That's the way it's always been in my disagreements with Sidney. He's either outright right or he's right even when he's wrong because you are "uptight."

It didn't relieve my guilt any that Sidney was hospitalized a few days later. He gave out at both ends. The parasites had coexisted with him in India, but in New York, they attacked. Ma Prem Isabel phoned to tell me Sidney was in the hospital. This deep voice with a French accent said over the phone, "He thought you ought to know."

I wasn't sure why. Wasn't she his wife? I wondered how she and Mildred Kantor were getting on, realizing with a shock that Mildred was now Ma Prem Isabel's mother-in-law, not mine. And who was paying the hospital bill? Sidney gave up his Blue Cross when he left Rutgers.

I visited Sidney at Mount Sinai. His eyes were glazed, his face sunken. He raised a stick-like hand from the counterpane in greeting. "Hello, Elaine," he whispered.

I was drawn to him even in this pitiful state. The sickness had made his eyes more beautiful. Even then I'd have taken him back, though I tried not to reveal that to him. A psychologist friend once said to me, "Sidney will only come back to you when you don't want him anymore." I'm ashamed to say I took satisfaction in knowing Sidney had never been sick like this when he was married to me.

Sidney was not only physically ill, he was psychologically down as well. He had no job, no existence other than as a disciple. What do you do when your profession is worshipping a guru and the guru isn't in residence?

Sidney looked helpless. Not that he admitted anything to me. "This must be hard for you," I observed.

"No," he said, repeating what must be the party line among the disciples, "This is just what is. I'm watching it. I'm making a meditation out of it."

I was tempted to say, "I hear ya."

Ma Prem Isabel came in. She was large and, I was sorry to admit, quite beautiful in a mannish way. Amidst the hospital whiteness, she looked like a pagan goddess in her dazzling orange outfit, red boots, and long black hair which hung down to her waist.

"Hello," she said, striding into the room like she owned it. "You must be Elaine." And before I could decide how to respond she came up to me, kissed me on the cheek, and said, "We must be friends."

Yes, I thought, acting as well as I could. How do you do, Ma Prem Isabel? I understand you are my husband's new wife. Sorry I couldn't attend the bridal shower, but India is a long way off.

I had Sidney and Ma Prem Isabel over to lunch when he got out of the hospital, if for no other reason than I didn't want to feel mean.

Everyone was on their best behavior. Ma Prem Isabel greeted me with her customary kiss on the cheek. And I acted well too. I had to. Jane watched me like a hawk; I was damned if I'd be the bad one.

Sidney acted as if he'd never been gone. He strode about in his orange garb, showing the house to Ma Prem Isabel like he was still lord of the manor. "This is where I had my wine cellar. And this is my study." He even got out the old photo albums and sat beside her on the couch showing her pictures of the children as they grew up.

"You have beautiful children," Ma Prem Isabel told me in a matter-of-fact way, again putting me at a disadvantage. Since she wasn't jealous of Sidney's past, I had to do my best not to appear jealous of his present.

Sidney wanted to show Ma Prem Isabel the Delaware and Raritan Canal, and he and Isabel (Lord, must I forever refer to her as "Ma Prem Isabel?") and Jane and Harry—who had just gotten off the school bus—went out back. From the kitchen window I watched them fade into the swampy woods—Sidney, Isabel, and Jane bright as tropical birds, Harry drab in blue jeans.

SOMETIMES WHEN I LOOK out over the fields into the woods, or walk down to the river, where the children built their clubhouse—it's still up in the tree, the boards grey now and warped—I think nothing has changed. Sidney is still here. The children are still small.

In Griggstown, the different parts and places in your life blend together. Griggstown is a quiet, green oasis in polluted New Jersey, a nineteenth-century backwater, forgotten. Yet, we're not really isolated, I tell myself. A person could get into a rowboat, float down the overgrown canal to New Brunswick, where it enters the Raritan, and follow the Raritan to the sea.

Griggstown gives rise to such musings. It's quiet and dreamy, and there's history all around and life never changes. Well, actually, it changes. Lord knows it changes. But Griggstown's bucolic constancy kept me sane over these years after my life came apart.

Can I help it if I'm a traditional woman? If Sidney didn't want a traditional woman, why did he marry me?

When am I going to give up this worthless fantasy that Sidney will someday crawl home begging forgiveness and everything will be as it was? Not only is he married to someone else now. Not only has he joined a cult. But if I'm to be honest with myself, it never *was* the way it was. It was always *going to be*.

Even in the beginning of our marriage there was something wrong. Sidney said he loved me but acted like he hated me. He would fly into these awful rages—what we called his "hatings"—when, sometimes for days at a time, he acted like he couldn't stand me. I would say, "What did I do?" But I never had done anything. I loved him. And something about that enraged him.

But, at least in the early days, when he came out of these rages, he was contrite. And I always believed it was something he would outgrow. That was the myth our relationship fed on: that someday it would be better.

Later, even the myth disappeared. The rages subsided but Sidney just ignored me. It was as if so much of his energy had gone into despising me that, when that ended, he wasn't sure who I was. Now there was nothing for me to look forward to. I just got older. And yet? How I wish Sidney were back. We may have been miserable, but that misery was the only life I had. Divorce brought just emptiness.

Divorce is like a great lingering death. No, it's worse than death. If someone close to you dies, well, it's terrible, but you get over it eventually. You have to. But how do you get over a death when the person who "died" is still walking around in your life?

For a while I went to this support group of formerly married men and women down the road in Princeton. It met every Friday evening at the Unitarian church. Ah, the Unitarians. Wednesday nights, chamber music. Thursday nights, Gay Men and Lesbian Women. Friday nights, the Formerly Married. Saturday nights, Swinging Singles. Eventually, I was told, the Formerly Married gravitated towards the Swinging Singles.

But I didn't go to the group long enough. I just couldn't stand it. I used to refer to Fridays as the "Night of the Living Dead."

Maybe people who haven't had children can get over a divorce easier.

The children—why did we have them? I mean, I love them dearly; they are my treasures. But Sidney and I never decided to have children. I just kept getting pregnant.

It was what people did in those days. Sidney and I kept conceiving, but we were never lovers. Our love life was fraught with tension. Sidney kept complaining about my orgasms. I didn't have orgasms. Or I didn't have the right kind of orgasms. Or I had too many orgasms.

I didn't care whether I had orgasms or not. I just wanted to be close to him.

Sidney also accused me of not knowing how to put in the diaphragm. "Well," I said to him, "if you think I'm doing it wrong, why don't you do it with me?"

That was a mistake. Sidney pretended he hadn't heard me say it, but, afterward, he didn't talk to me for a week. Sidney was always campaigning for openness, for nudity, for free everything, but the body disgusted him. If one of the kids had a nosebleed, Sidney went for a walk. When he used the upstairs toilet, everyone had to remain downstairs.

Once I surprised Sidney in our bedroom, gingerly holding my diaphragm aloft and shining a flashlight through it. He held the diaphragm like it was a diseased clam. "What are you doing?" I asked.

"There are holes in it," he said, looking at me accusingly.

Sidney had known someone in graduate school whose wife gave birth to four children, including twins, before confessing she had made holes in her diaphragm. Her husband hadn't wanted children, so she conceived them on the sly.

Sidney said the woman had committed the ultimate crime, what Nathaniel Hawthorne called a crime against the human heart. "That woman stole his seed," Sidney said. "She raped him."

I wasn't sure about rape, but otherwise, I fully shared Sidney's horror and told him so. Now he seemed to believe I had done the same thing to him.

I went to the gynecologist the next day, taking the diaphragm with me. He assured me there was nothing wrong with it and that I was inserting it correctly. "It just doesn't work all the time," he said.

When I told Sidney this he shrugged. "We both know what you're doing" he said.

"What?" I said. "What am I doing?"

But he wouldn't say more than that. And afterwards, he almost never wanted to have sex.

I got pregnant anyway, and we'd have had a third child if not for the abortion. It was Sidney's idea. He didn't demand I get an abortion but he let me know, in his inimitable way, that he would leave me if I didn't. I wished I'd kept the baby. Sidney left me anyway.

After my abortion Sidney got a vasectomy. When he told me he was going to do it I thought, He loves me after all. How could I have been so naive? He didn't get that vasectomy for me. He got it to sleep with every woman he could get his hands on up at the university.

Sidney's vasectomy became his calling card. Ling Po said Sidney let her know about it during their first conversation in his office. He even mentioned it in his classes. Oh, he'd slyly disguise it in talk of contemporary sex roles or whatnot, but the message he was telegraphing to all those nubile young women was, "Hey, *I* won't get you pregnant."

THESE WERE MY THOUGHTS as I stared out the kitchen window and waited for them to come back from the canal. True to form, Sidney had said they'd be back in fifteen minutes and, stupid me, I took him at his word and had their blessed vegetarian lunch laid out. The salad was wilting, the bread getting stale, the homemade soup boiling over on the stove. It had been an hour already. My God, I thought, he's kidnapped Harry. He already had Jane and now he's taken Harry. When I finally spotted them approaching the house through the woods, I was relieved to see Harry still dressed in blue.

After lunch, Sidney and Ma Prem Isabel stayed on, saying nothing about leaving. The sun started down. It got dark and they were still here. I guess they had nowhere to go, nothing to do. The ashramites had dispersed throughout the world and were marking time until the word came down from on high as to where the new ashram would be. My feelings about Sidney careened back and forth between anger and pity.

I served tea. Or, I tried to. Lipton's wasn't good enough; it had to be rosehips or dandelions or something. Harry said— looking disdainfully at me for not having any on hand— that he would get some herbal tea, and before I could say no, had "liberated" —as he liked to put it— the car keys and was tearing out of the driveway on the way to the store. Harry, who had recently lost his driver's license for a year.

I remained calm. Harry could probably get to the store undetected by the police and without destroying the car or himself. I just had to get through the afternoon.

After tea Sidney finally said they ought to leave. Thank God. But they had no transportation back to New Brunswick, where they were now staying with George and, as Sidney put it, his "significant other" in the old apartment on Church Street. Sidney and Isabel had hitchhiked out to Griggstown, but hitchhiking back wouldn't be possible in the dark. Would I give them a ride? Well, it was that or let Harry take them, so I took them; but I kept thinking, Why does Sidney put me in these positions? If he wants to be an impoverished orange person and give up having a car, why do I have to drive him places?

Ma Prem Isabel embraced Jane and Harry. "Isn't she terrific?" Harry opined as we got into the car. I kept my face straight.

Living in the country you do a lot of carpooling and chauffeuring, but it was a unique experience chauffeuring an ex-husband and his wife, who sat in the back holding hands and laughing like teenagers. Who was I, their mother?

I took Canal Road up to New Brunswick to avoid the traffic. It's neat in there along the canal. The New Jersey Turnpike runs just a few miles to the east, but on Canal Road you've got to watch out for deer. The canal's walls are caving in, and bass leap among the lily pads growing in the shallows. If not for the occasional locktender's house and the rusting machinery, you'd think the canal was a river.

Taking a break from the revelries in the back seat, Sidney suggested I get the car tuned. "It's idling rough," he said. Sidney probably thought he was being helpful, doing me a big favor. Who needs your opinion? I wanted to say. I've kept this car going for two years without your help, so why get into the act now?

When we got to Church Street, Sidney invited me upstairs. I said I didn't have time, but he knew better.

I didn't want to go up there. I'd had enough pain without revisiting the scene of Sidney's conquests. After Ling Po's visit I went there in a vain attempt to get Sidney to come home and had to listen to George Smith being profound. "You're not responsible for Sidney's life," George said, sounding just like Sidney.

While George talked I had stood around paralyzed, wondering, Was that the bed where Sidney made love to Ling Po? Were there other Ling Pos? Would I ever be able to come up to New Brunswick and the university without cringing every time someone snickered, for fear they were laughing at me?

There is a word for men in my position: cuckold. I felt as cuckolded as any man. There wasn't just pain in Sidney's unfaithfulness; there was shame. Words to the country song, "Couldn't Hold

Her Man," hounded me day and night. I'd wake in the middle of the night in a sweat, the music throbbing in my brain.

Sidney insisted I come upstairs, and I decided what the heck. It was about time I exorcised the ghosts of that apartment. The apartment was very different from what I remembered. George and Steve had uncovered classic moldings and medallions above what had been a false ceiling and installed stained glass windows and art nouveau chandeliers. Plants trailed about the windows and a Paul Berthon print and a Lalique vase on a delicate shelf, graced the walls. When Sidney lived there it was a pigsty.

George and Steve were home and welcomed me with what seemed excessive enthusiasm. I suspected I had more than once been the subject of comment in this apartment since Sidney and Isabel arrived a few days ago.

Sidney brought me some wine. He kept acting as if nothing tragic, or even difficult, had ever passed between us. Our divorce was the disaster of my life, but Sidney seemed eager to demonstrate it hadn't really changed anything. Oh yes, he had another wife, but I was still, in some sense, his wife. He was courteous to the point of being seductive. Indeed, he was nicer than I could ever remember him being.

I wondered what Ma Prem Isabel thought about this, but she seemed to accept Sidney's attentions to me as natural. She was handmaiden to what seemed the prevailing wisdom in that room: that we were all great friends.

I suppose there was something noble about it. Why should divorced people hate the person they were once closest to in the whole world? Why not be friends? George and Sandy had managed it. Couldn't I be a little less conventional, a little more open-minded?

Only, that wasn't the way it truly felt in that apartment. It may have been the agreed-upon agenda or ideology of the other four, but I don't know if they really believed it. And I certainly didn't.

What can I say? I'm not groovy. I don't believe in—or, at least, I'm not capable of—socializing happily with ex-husbands and their new wives. And while I'm for gay people being themselves, I don't know why George Smith, who used to be married to my friend Sandy, had to pick this time to neck in the corner of the living room with his lover. Give me a break, George.

My efforts at flexibility weren't aided by the photograph of Sidney and Ma Prem Isabel, nude, which was framed and hanging in a prominent place. Sidney was giving the camera the finger, as they say. I had been looking at George and Steve's paintings and prints when I noticed the photograph amongst them. What was my response supposed to be? Do ex-wives have to look at photographs of ex-husbands and their new wives in the nude with total equanimity and good grace? The truth is, the photograph made me slightly nauseous. There was something obscene about it. Not the photograph itself but my being forced to look at it. What was I supposed to say, "Right on Sidney!"? If my reactions to looking at that photograph betrayed my midwest Methodist origins, so be it. I wondered if Sidney had invited me up to the apartment specifically to see this photograph, his idea of a good joke I was supposed to share.

Sidney came and put his arm around me as I looked at the picture, trapping me there when I would have preferred nobody knew I had even seen it. Why was he being so affectionate? He kissed me on the cheek. Was he trying to torture me, antagonize Isabel, or both?

Everyone was drinking; we seemed to be having a party. Two gay men, an ex-husband and his new wife, and me torn between fleeing that place immediately or getting into the spirit of things.

But what was the spirit of things? We sat on the couch now, Sidney with his arm around me. With every gesture he communicated to me that while he was married to Ma Prem Isabel, universal love was the ticket. Even ex-spouses were fair game. And Isabel seemed to be rooting for us. I wasn't sure whether to be pleased or disgusted.

Finally, I whispered to Sidney, "Please take your arm off me." He did, with that characteristic gesture of his which suggests — Well, if you're not cool, that's your problem — and went over to sit with Isabel.

Universal love, my foot! Whom are you kidding, Sidney? Once, when Sidney was living with George in New Brunswick, he suddenly burst through my door. Two nights before, George's ex-wife Sandy had fixed me up with her brother, Richard Sampson who was visiting from Iowa. We had spent a quiet evening at dinner and the movies, and somehow Sidney had heard about it. Sidney had been urging me to see other men, but the first time I did he came storming home to Griggstown. He didn't mention my date once, but he stalked about, discussing *his* house, *his* wife, *his* children, *his* land. I had never seen him so patriarchal, so hot instead of cool. I rather liked it.

But this mood lasted only three days. Then, as if ashamed at his outburst of feelings, Sidney returned to the apartment in New Brunswick and never came home to stay again.

Now he was lying with his head in Isabel's lap, pointedly ignoring me. George turned on the 10 P.M. news, perhaps to cover the tension in the room. There were stories about murders in Brooklyn and Jersey City. There was an interview with President Reagan in which he argued for prayer in the schools. Then, after the sports, there was what the television anchor called a "human interest" story.

Babadahs filled the screen. "Look," Ma Prem Isabel cried. All attention was riveted to the screen. The camera zoomed in on Babadahs sitting in a trance.

The newscaster said, "The disciples of Babadahs, believing him to be God's emissary on earth, have purchased a hundred-square-mile ranch in desolate eastern Oregon where a commune will be built. The reported price: six million dollars.

"Living until recently in India, where they have encountered what they characterize as 'persecution,' Babadahs and his disciples have decided to transfer their activities to this 75,000-acre ranch [the camera panned over the desert country] where John Wayne's movie *Big Muddy* was filmed."

The news program included footage of a small group of disciples living in a mobile home that had been trucked into the ranch. "It's great," someone called Ma Sangeet, formerly Toby O'Reilly, said in a southern accent when asked by the television reporter what an Indian guru was doing in the American wilderness.

People in Buffalo, the nearest town to the ranch—twenty miles away, with a population of forty—were less enthusiastic. "We believe in freedom of religion," the mayor of the near ghost town said, "but does he?"

The instant the broadcast ended, Sidney rushed to the bookcase and got out an atlas. "Buffalo," he muttered. "Buffalo." His finger moved over the map of Oregon. "Where the hell is Buffalo?"

He finally located it about one hundred fifty miles east of Portland. "Lord," he said, "Here it is. In the middle of absolutely, unbelievably nowhere."

"Buffalo," Sidney kept saying. "Incredible. The ashram isn't coming to America. It's coming to *America!* Cowboys. Only now it's going to be cowboys and Indians."

Sidney and Ma Prem Isabel were jumping up and down and hugging each other. Then they were hugging George and Steve. Then, before I could escape, they were hugging me. "Buffalo," Sidney kept saying in wonderment. "'Oh, give me a home . . . .'"

Babadahs brought out a side of Sidney I had rarely seen. Sidney was like an excited boy scout who had just been told by the troop leader where he was going on the next camping trip. "Buffalo," he kept saying. "Far freaking out."

Maybe that was the trouble with our marriage: being the kind of female I am, I had wanted Sidney to be strong. Babadahs let him be a little boy. And Ma Prem Isabel was so robust, Sidney so skinny, he looked like her son as she hugged him against herself.

With all the merriment in the room I thought I might safely leave. Before I went downstairs, Sidney asked if we might have lunch some day. I was wary of seeing him. I almost preferred now to see him *with* Ma Prem Isabel. But to get out of there, I agreed. After all, he would soon be leaving for Babadahspuram, as the commune was to be called. He would be out of my life again.

And I wanted him out of my life. Mostly, anyway. While he was in India I had taken the first tentative steps towards putting myself back together again. I took graduate courses in English at Rutgers. Sometimes I saw a man. Sidney's appearance on the scene had disrupted all that. My continuing attraction for him made me uncertain, ambivalent, unable to breathe.

To make matters worse, Sidney wasn't yet invited to be a resident of Babadahspuram; they had no need for his skills. Jane, on the other hand, was wanted out there immediately to continue with her personnel work; all disciple records were going to be computerized. I remember thinking, Well, that's a skill she can use whenever she gives up this Babadahs business.

Isabel also left for Oregon. In India, she had worked as a carpenter, and they needed carpenters in Oregon. Sidney was left behind, still uncertain about his future. What if he were never invited to Oregon?

He continued living with George in the shadow of Rutgers, with no position, no money, nothing to do all day—a strange, orange street person. I resisted the impulse to call him, even though sometimes I shamelessly fantasized that, with Isabel out of town, well . . . .

I would steel myself to resist Sidney by saying the last thing I needed was someone like Sidney in my life. I had no idea what kind of man would suit me, but one word kept popping into my head: ordinary. A shoe salesman. An orthodontist. Anything but far out.

Sandy Smith's brother came through New Jersey for a visit again. Richard Sampson is a systems analyst, whatever that is, who lives in Des Moines, Iowa. Stocky. On the boring side. But sweet, considerate, kind. No trips. He opened doors for me. He brought me flowers.

We had dinner at J. August's cafe in New Brunswick. Afterwards we went for a drive, ending up in Johnson Park, overlooking the Raritan River. Richard put his arm around me. "I hope you won't mind if I kiss you," he said.

Mind? We necked. I felt fifteen again. I had to be careful not to scare him away.

We made a date to see each other two days later. Richard started the car and we drove through New Brunswick on our way to Griggstown.

As we came down George Street I noticed a commotion a block ahead. There was fighting going on. Loud voices. Someone got hit and fell to the ground.

As we pulled alongside, I saw it was Sidney. In his orange outfit he looked like a broken harlequin.

"Stop the car, Richard," I said.

"It's only a derelict," Richard said, continuing on.

"Stop the car!"

I was out before Richard had parked. A gang of teenagers surrounded Sidney. One had his foot on Sidney's chest, holding him down. Another was going through his wallet. "Let's see what the orange motherfucker has," I heard him say.

"Get away from him," I yelled as I approached.

Richard was just behind me. "Elaine, come away from here. Elaine, you've got no business here."

At the sight of burly Richard, the kids ran. Richard looks like an FBI man.

Sidney was unconscious and bleeding from a gash on his head. "Come on," I said, "we've got to get him to a hospital."

"Elaine," Richard insisted, "let's call the police. Let them take care of this. It's not our business."

"It's *my* business," I replied.

"But Elaine, this guy's a bum."

"No he isn't," I said. "He's my husband. Ex-husband," I quickly corrected, but my mistake wasn't lost on Richard. He picked Sidney up like a doll and reluctantly placed him on the back seat of the car, where Sidney bled on the upholstery. We drove to Robert Wood Johnson University Hospital.

Richard stayed with me in the waiting area of the emergency room, but he obviously couldn't wait to get away from there. He was slowly distancing himself from me. "How could you have been married to such a kook?" he whispered.

Richard didn't keep his date with me two days later. He called to say he had to get back to Des Moines early. "I'll call you," he said, but I didn't expect he would.

That was okay. In that moment on the sidewalk in New Brunswick, I had seen that my future didn't lie with the Richards of this world after all. Despite the pain and horror, Sidney had at least been interesting. But aren't there interesting men around who aren't crazy?

I met Sidney on a blind date when we were both in college. I was a freshman at the University of Massachusetts in Amherst, trying to shed my farmgirl ways. Sidney was a senior at Amherst College. Every girl at UMass wanted to go out with a boy from Amherst College. They were considered real catches.

"You'll like him," my roommate said. "He's different."

I'll say he was different. All the other college guys were animals. They tried to jump on top of me five minutes after we met. They'd say "Hello" and start tearing off my blouse.

That's how it went with John Rafferty, Sidney's roommate. I was fixed up with him some weeks before. "A regular guy," my roommate said.

After all the "regular" guys, Sidney was a relief. He was quiet, soulful. He seemed to want me to do the talking, and he listened to me like no man had ever listened to me before. Everything I said seemed to fascinate him. I'd tell him ordinary things and his eyes grew wide with amazement. He made me feel good.

He made no attempt to kiss me at all on our first date. Nor on our second. Sidney was the only man I had gone out with who wasn't in a hurry to both make a million dollars and get my panties off. I remember thinking he was the gentlest man I'd ever met. He was elegant. He had manners.

Men didn't like Sidney much. He didn't play sports, didn't belong to a fraternity, didn't care about being a big man on campus. Sidney was truly a ladies man. He even delighted my anti-Semitic mother. "You know," mother said when Sidney and I flew out to Nebraska just before we got married, "Jesus was a Jew," as if this revelation, which had just come to her, made our marriage tolerable. Sidney was clever and charming and funny with mother. He was clever and charming and funny with all women, that was the problem.

Sidney was ahead of his time. His style would flourish in the seventies, the heyday of the "sensitive man." No wonder our marriage fell apart in the seventies.

I can remember going with him to a party at Rutgers in the early seventies. Every woman in the room knew Sidney. Every one of them seemed to think she had a special relationship with him. It gave me the creeps.

Later, I learned lots of them *did* have a special relationship with him—students, professors, even a lady dean. For Sidney, women's liberation became the foolproof way to get women into bed. He'd wring his hands about being a chauvinist pig, he'd put on his vulnerable look, and, the *coup de grace*, he'd cry. The crying got them if nothing else did. Women were desperate to take care of Sidney.

That's the way it was between him and me. On our third date we drove out to Harkins Mountain and parked. Sidney didn't say anything, just stared at me. He had this enormous ability to pay attention, to make you feel nothing like this had ever happened before.

I melted. I leaned over and kissed him. I'd never done that before with a boy, taken the initiative.

Sidney kept staring.

I kissed him again. I opened my blouse and put his hand inside.

I had grown up in a world of dire warnings about petting above the waist and petting below the waist. Sidney seduced me by just looking at me.

Or, rather, I seduced him. I zipped open his fly and took him in my hand. Then into my mouth. Little Elaine Montgomery from North Forks, Nebraska!

Every boy I'd ever been out with had wanted me to do that to him. "If you loved me you would suck it just a little." "Please do it or I'll be hospitalized." I can still remember all that pressure on my neck.

But with Sidney.... How can I put it? Sidney let me have my way with him.

I loved having sex with Sidney. That's why I married him. But after we got married I'd often wonder, Did he love having sex with me? I never felt I quite satisfied him. It's as if he was somehow above sex, as if he was too great a man for ordinary pursuits. His orgasms were private. He just went inside himself, as if there were part of him he didn't want me to see.

He'd never say, "That was great, Elaine," or "That was beautiful, Elaine," or "I love you, Elaine." He especially didn't say "I love you, Elaine." He had some vague notion that saying "I love you" was dishonest. I tried not to say it too often to him.

I don't know why Sidney married me. I married him because I'd always thought I was shy and inhibited, but with Sidney I was a sex fiend. You can imagine what a novelty that was in the beginning.

I always took the initiative in our lovemaking. I even proposed. Sidney said, "Sure." He agreed to marry me like he agreed to have sex.

Early in our relationship I took Sidney's manner as vulnerability. Sidney was soft. He was open.

Later, I came to see his openness as a trap. Sidney never offered anything, never extended himself. He got you to extend yourself, and he kept backing up, retreating. I'd think: this man needs me. He's shy; he's afraid. He values my opinion. And BAM!—he'd give it to me good.

Sidney only appears to be gentle. His is the gentleness of the assassin.

All the years of our relationship I danced around him, and he'd watch me, not commenting. I never learned to stop taking his silence for compliance or even support. Then, with one cutting remark, Sidney would destroy me.

Sidney is the master of the putdown. He's so good at putting you down you don't even know you've been put down. Sometimes it took me days to figure it out.

I never had a way of truly getting back at him, never. Sidney's three-times smarter than me.

Or maybe he just had three times more schooling than me. When we got married I quit school and got a job. That was called the Ph.T. in those days: Putting Hubby Through. It was an honorable profession. And it wouldn't have been such a bad deal if it had worked. You were the breadwinner now; he would be the breadwinner later. And along the way he would pass on to you as many educational goodies as possible.

Oh, but it doesn't work that way. People aren't grateful for what you do for them. They owe you, and it makes them angry. When Sidney got his doctorate and became a professor I was proud of him, but whatever part I'd had in it only made him antagonistic toward me later. Damn it, maybe *I* should have become the professor.

It wouldn't have been so bad if Sidney had shared his learning with me. But what was his was his. Despite all his solidarity with students and workers and the poor and the ill-educated and all the world's deprived, Sidney looked down at me for my lack of education.

Then it got worse because Sidney became an anti-intellectual intellectual. I had worshipped at the shrine of education, but here was Sidney, high priest of that shrine, saying it was worthless.

This put more distance between us. Now Sidney wasn't just more educated than me. He was above education. Sidney was always erecting new superstructures which left me still lower down.

While I languished at home, Sidney did "in" things. He went off to march in Selma, Alabama. He attended anti-Vietnam marches, women's rights marches, gay rights marches, anti-nuclear marches. Sidney was always there. But he never took me with him.

Instead of sharing with me, Sidney made demands. Why didn't I join a fashionable feminist rap group? There was status for him in having a wife who was a member of a feminist group and, Goddamit, I should get into one.

Sidney was always managing me. Why didn't I wear miniskirts? Okay, I started wearing them, keeping up with his teenyboppers at the university as best I could. Then he wanted me to wear tights—probably to cover up my varicose veins, but he didn't say. "You've got to grow," Sidney was always saying. Believe me, I grew. I grew.

But there were limits. Sidney thought I was dull because I didn't go to therapists all the time. Sidney went to a prodigious number of therapists.

Now his guru says the only important thing is to accept yourself exactly as you are. I could have told him that twenty years ago. I *did* tell him that twenty years ago.

Sidney confused anxiety with intelligence. His notion was that if a person wasn't anxious he was stupid, insensitive. I remember Sidney saying that George Smith was a sensitive person.

"Maybe he's just gay," I said.

My relationship with Sidney consisted in trying desperately to live up to his expectations. Only those expectations constantly shifted.

Sidney always kept me off balance. He was always coming up with what I came to call his sexual schemes. Whatever was non-conventional in sex interested him. For Sidney, sex was a head trip.

One year his big interest was fantasies. He wanted us to tell each other our sexual fantasies. He thought that would make our marriage honest. "Honesty" was a big word with Sidney. "Honesty" and "sincerity" and "let it all hang out."

He'd say, "See that blond over there? Boy, would I ever love to part her thighs."

Not only would he say things like that, he'd look to me for approval. As if he deserved applause for his honesty.

What was I to say to such a thing? Thank you? I hated his fantasies. It was bad enough he had them; did he have to assault me with them?

Sidney had the notion that through sharing our fantasies we would remain faithful to each other. "If I can tell you my fantasies, then I won't have to carry them out," he would say. I was supposed to listen to this stuff and be grateful.

None of it felt like honesty to me. It felt like a threat. I would cringe whenever Sidney began to tell me a fantasy.

You'd think I'd have demanded equal time, given him some of his own medicine. But I almost never did. It wasn't my style. Besides, I was so terrified of his fantasies, I stopped having any of my own. It was as if part of my mind had clicked off, knowing that if I had fantasies and told him about them, I'd have to listen to more of his.

Sidney was always dragging oddball ideas into our marriage. And, somehow, it developed that I became the conservative one, the prude, the naysayer. I don't know how I got into that position, but there I was.

Sidney brought home the O'Neills' book *Open Marriage* and left it prominently on our bedside table for weeks. He felt we should read it and discuss it.

"Look Sidney," I said, "if what you're saying is that you want to have affairs, don't expect my approval."

"I don't want to have affairs," Sidney would insist. "I want to talk about things."

I felt like a pincushion. I never knew what Sidney would stick me with next. Or where.

He went out to California one year during the university's spring break and spent a week at Esalen. He returned with a picture of himself and some men and women nude in a hot-tub. I kept my feelings about that to myself.

But he kept needling me. I just had to read Carl Rogers. I just had to read Fritz Perls.

I read a Carl Rogers book. It was full of case histories of couples who have had affairs and now are madly in love with each other. I've never known anyone like that. The marriages I know where there have been affairs are either dead or the people still in them are like cancer patients, dragging themselves around with half their organs.

Sidney showed me "The Gestalt Prayer" in a Fritz Perls book:

I do my thing, and you do your thing.
I am not in this world to live up to your expectations.
And you are not in this world to live up to mine.
You are you and I am I.
And if by chance we find each other, it's beautiful.
If not, it can't be helped.

Sidney liked the Gestalt Prayer so much he sent off to California for a plastic plaque as a present for me. I put the Perls plaque on the shelf in the back of my closet, but Sidney found it there one day and stuck it on the refrigerator with magnets. I had to look at it every time I reached for the orange juice.

Sidney took a great interest in communes and multiple marriage. He read Robert Rimmer's *Proposition 31,* about two couples who form a four-person marriage. For a while it was his Bible. Then Sidney visited The Farm, in Summertown, Tennessee, a large commune famous for its multiple marriages. Sidney came back entranced. "They have marriages down there with three people in it, four people in it, five people. It's great." Sidney thought anything was great but what we had.

One night, when George and Sandy Smith were over and we'd been drinking a lot of wine, Sidney got talking about The Farm and *Proposition 31.* "Don't you think the nuclear family is unnatural?" Sidney asked. "Maybe the four of us could combine households."

Sidney had some notion of building a covered walkway between our two houses. This would integrate them architecturally. Then, Sidney thought, we could begin to integrate them economically. Only one of us would have to worry about finances. Only one of us would have to shop. Dinners would be eaten alternately in the two houses. "That would get us together once a day," Sidney said.

George was fascinated. George was always fascinated by Sidney's schemes.

Then Sidney said offhandedly, "Of course, eventually, we might become integrated sexually too."

There was dead silence.

"Well, we'd need to think about that," Sandy said.

"Nothing to think about," Sidney said. "We'd just have to work out a system so everything'd be cool."

I said I thought Sidney's idea would destroy the friendship the four of us shared. "There'll be blood all over Griggstown."

Sidney said I was a prude. "If people are really friends," he said, "they share everything. Sexual jealousy isn't natural," he insisted. "We feel it because we're supposed to. There's that sign on the wall saying: 'Thou shalt not commit adultery.' Let's put up our own sign."

"Watch this now," Sidney said. He walked over to where Sandy Smith was sitting on the couch. He sat down next to her, put his arms around her, and kissed her long and hard. "Tell the truth," Sidney said, coming up for air, "does this bother anyone or do you just think you should be bothered?"

Everyone looked at George to see what he thought. That was back when none of us knew George was gay. Here was George, tortured by desires to sleep with men, and Sidney suggesting he start sleeping with not one but two women.

"What do you think, Sandy?" George asked, passing the buck.

"I'm just catching my breath," Sandy said noncommittally.

I knew what I thought. As soon as George and Sandy went home I hit Sidney with the heel of my grey suede pump. It raised an enormous lump. Later I realized I could have killed him hitting him like that. And, still later, I wished I had.

"What'd you hit me for?" Sidney complained. "You know I don't believe in violence."

"Don't believe in violence?" I cried. "What do you call what went on in our living room a little while ago?"

"Make love not war," Sidney said.

"For you, love *is* war," I replied.

Sidney wouldn't drop the subject of multiple marriage. We got as far as two dinners, one at our house and one at the Smiths'. It wasn't too different from the dinners we occasionally shared anyway, but now there was tension in the air. Was this the beginning of combined households? Would the sexual stuff follow?

After the two dinners the project didn't go anywhere. The Smiths and I never pushed the subject, and Sidney was too flighty to stay with one idea very long. He was already off on some other hare-brained scheme. For a while he lobbied for a trip to Plato's Retreat, the orgy place in New York.

Occasionally, Sidney resurrected the multiple marriage idea in some form. One time he said to me, as if this were a plus, that sometimes the women in multiple marriages have sex with each other. Sidney was all in favor of it. He said he loved women so much that in his next incarnation, he was coming back as a lesbian and having lots of affairs with women.

Sidney thought I ought to have a lesbian affair. "It's perfectly all right with me" he said.

"I don't want to have a lesbian affair," I insisted.

"Yes you do," he'd say. "You just won't admit it to yourself."

That was Sidney all over. Saying you didn't want something was proof you wanted it for sure. You were covering up, repressing.

Sidney said if I ever had a lesbian affair I could be perfectly open about it. "You could do it right in front of me," he said. It almost felt like Sidney was demanding I do it in front of him.

Ironically, after George became openly homosexual and left Sandy, she made a kind of awkward pass at me. Sandy was so broken up about George being homosexual she thought she must be homosexual too.

I had always wondered whether something happened between Sidney and Sandy after their clinch in our living room. They probably thought about it for a while. One time Sidney was over the Smith's house for a few hours and, I later learned, George had been out of town.

But here was Sandy coming on to me. It was Saturday night, and we were alone. Sidney was already spending a lot of time with George in New Brunswick. Sandy and I always hugged each other hello and goodbye. But this time, when Sandy hugged me, she didn't let go.

"Don't be silly, Sandy," I said.

Sandy looked at me then, good and hard. "You're right," she said. "Yuck." Those were the days when everyone was coming out of the closet. And not just coming out of the closet; they were hiring halls.

Each day there were fresh revelations. This movie star. That professional athlete. There was even speculation about a certain president of the United States. Astronauts.

Frankly, I don't care if people do it with birds as long as the birds are adult consenting birds. But society was being positively bludgeoned with people's gayness.

This was particularly true around the university. You couldn't go to a party at Rutgers without someone you'd known for years saying in the most matter-of-fact way, "Of course that was before I came out of the closet."

Bill Martin, of the Psychology Department, said that to me. What was I to say? I'd never known he was in the closet. The last time I'd seen Bill Martin was when his son William went to the junior high prom with Jane, and Bill drove them.

Sidney thought all this public confession was wonderful. "Maximizing the love," he'd say.

Love. What did he know about love? Sidney's never loved anybody. Of course he loves Sidney. The one body that obsesses him is
his own.

What a hypochondriac he is. Always sitting around with a ther-
mometer in his mouth. Doctoring himself elaborately every time
he has a minor cut.

Sidney spent a fortune on vitamins. And not ordinary vitamins
either: the expensive ones sold in health boutiques. They come in
little plastic boxes with sliding tops, the kind fishermen keep dry
flies and lures in. Sidney was forever rattling open one of these
boxes and popping an oily vitamin.

When Sidney had a cold he infected the air with his misery. If he
had a simple ache he would get a massage.

Sidney never exerted himself. He never did anything unless he
thought "the vibes were right." He'd mow the lawn for half an hour
and contemplate it for two.

I remember when Sidney started losing his hair. He couldn't
believe it, that this was happening *to him*. He'd stand by the mirror
in the bathroom by the hour, parting his hair this way and that,
holding a hand mirror so as to be able to see his head from all angles.
He was sure he had a disease.

He grew his beard when his hair started falling out. It was as if he
were trying to coax the hair from his face up onto his head.

I would reassure him all the time. "You're a very handsome man,
Sidney," I would say. "What's a little hair?"

"What's a little hair?" he would scream. Sidney regarded with
suspicion my finding him handsome as ever. Perhaps I was responsible for his hair loss.

"It's your eyes that have always attracted me to you, Sidney," I
would say. "I don't even look at your hair."

"Don't talk about my eyes when I may have cancer of the scalp,"
he shouted.

Losing some of his hair may have accelerated Sidney's desire for
a nonconventional lifestyle. Perhaps he thought it was now or
never. Make hay while your hair's still on your head.

He became wild. Then he became weird. Only there's an irony
in his being a Babadahs disciple. He's finally achieved major oddball status—but he and all the other disciples are just like each other. It's like a club. They talk the same, they wear the same uniform.

One day Sidney will wake up to the fact that he gave away his life for nothing. I wouldn't care to be near him at that moment.

Sidney looked happy enough when I visited him in the hospital the day after he got beat up. Being hurt gave him a certain status, gave him something to do. He was joking with his nurses, lapping up the attention, when I came in.

When he got out of the hospital he called to thank me for helping him—who do you think ended up paying his hospital bill?—and said he wanted to take me to lunch. We agreed to meet in Tumulty's Pub in New Brunswick the very next afternoon.

That was a mistake. First, Sidney arrived late. Not knowing what to do while I waited for him, I sat in a dark booth and ordered a Campari and soda. Men stared at me.

Sidney walked in when a big, open-shirted Italian, lots of gold chains tangled in his chest hair, was trying to pick me up. "Oh, I didn't mean to intrude," Sidney said. I noticed the flicker of interest in his eyes. His ex-wife, the sexpot.

The man stared contemptuously at Sidney's orange outfit and his mala with the picture of Babadahs. Sidney looked like a medieval court jester, like something out of an early Fellini movie.

"My husband," I said to break the tension. It seemed easier and more effective than saying my "ex-husband." The man retreated, looking both of us over, unsure which was stranger, Sidney or the fact I was "married" to such a person. I could hear him talking about us at the bar. "Did you get a load of that guy?" he said, gesturing over his shoulder with his thumb.

Sidney didn't appear to hear him. "Well," he said, smiling, fairly licking his lips. "Well," he repeated, as if it was perfectly all right with him that I hung out in bars and picked up men.

"You're half an hour late, Sidney," I said.

He didn't respond. Love means not ever having to say you're sorry or something like that. Sidney just looked at me, smiling.

"What do you want, Sidney?" I said.

Sidney called over the waiter and ordered lunch. "What's the best red wine you have?" Sidney asked the waiter and, without inquiring the price, said, "Bring it. We're celebrating."

"What are we celebrating?" I asked.

"Now," Sidney said. "We're celebrating *Now*."

Sidney said Babadahs preaches that the past is dead, the future may not happen. The only reality is "this very moment."

Babadahs also preaches that morality is situational. "What's moral is what's moral right now," Sidney said, putting his hand on mine.

There it was again, Sidney being seductive.

"What do you want, Sidney?" I repeated, not wishing to appear prudish but slipping my hand out from under his. I had slept with the man for twenty years, but now his touch felt like incest. Or worse.

"What I *want*," Sidney said, his eyes flashing angrily, "is for you to stop calling me Sidney!" I wondered how much *he* believed in his new name, how much he used it as a weapon.

After a moment Sidney softened. "That's what I wanted just then," he said. "What I want now is to get things straight between us."

"Straight." That was always a key word in Sidney's lexicon when we were married. He was forever suggesting we get things straight between us. Our marriage was a disaster, but we were always on the verge of getting things straight.

Of course straight always meant my accepting Sidney's version of reality. When I did, there was peace for a while. Things were straight between us.

But what was there to get straight between us in our present condition? "Isn't everything perfectly straight already?" I said. "We met. We married. We had two children. We got divorced. It all seems straight to me."

"No," Sidney said, cocking his head to one side, which gives him the appearance of vulnerability. "It isn't straight between us because of your anger."

Sidney proposed talking out our feelings towards each other. "*All* of them," he insisted.

I thought about that for a while. Sidney is a cobra and I'm a mouse. I can't deal with Sidney. The only way for me to deal with Sidney is to not deal with Sidney.

But I certainly had plenty of anger towards him, and anger is never pleasant. I don't know how to be angry at somebody without taking it out on myself. I get angry, I get depressed. If talking things out would relieve me of the burden of anger, it would be worth doing for that alone.

Sidney proposed certain rules. One of us would talk for half an hour while the other listened without interrupting. Then roles would be reversed for half an hour. Neither would comment on what the other said. The point was just to listen and, as Sidney put it, "see where the other person is coming from."

Sidney said this procedure had been used in relationship counseling at the ashram. "You'll see," he said. "At the end we'll have a complete understanding."

What a sucker I am. Why did I agree to go first? I allowed myself to be persuaded Sidney was being gallant by suggesting I go first. Now I see it was just his way of remaining in control.

I couldn't help it: I told Sidney everything. I mean *everything!* I laid myself wide open. I told him how betrayed and abandoned I felt. I told him I had loved him — that I still loved him.

I think I even — yes, I *did;* I don't want to lie about this — I actually told him that, despite everything, I would take him back. Oh, I want to throw up!

Sidney listened expressionless, eyeing me. He ordered another bottle of wine, which we sipped with dessert.

Finally, it was his turn. "Of course I love you too," he began. I waited for the "but." There has always been a but in Sidney's feelings for me. Now it came: "But everything you've said is absolutely totally unbelievable."

He didn't say "unbelievable to me." He just said "unbelievable." As if anyone with half a brain would know it was unbelievable.

Not to mention that Sidney was at once breaking his rule of no commentary on the other's ideas. Sidney, who used to say "I hear ya," only heard ya when it suited him.

Sidney proceeded to give his version of reality. I listened, amazed. Did he really believe this stuff? To sum up Sidney's point of view, I was responsible for the failure of our marriage. My anger over his abusing me for twenty years did it.

Sidney glossed over his massive infidelities as "just being playful." He said he did it for me, to help loosen me up; it was a necessary sacrifice on his part. He wouldn't have done it if I hadn't been "so possessive." Nothing like blaming the victim.

Sidney went on to describe his "pain when I came home and found you had been dating another man."

I forgot myself and shouted, "What other man? What are you talking about?" Sidney reminded me I was not to talk during his half hour.

Sidney said our marriage "collapsed" because of my first date (if that was what it was) with Richard Sampson several years before. I didn't know whether to be amused or cry. "And then to see you with that same guy the other night as I lay helpless on the sidewalk. Talk about dancing on someone's grave . . . ." Sidney actually seemed sorry for himself.

Sidney also blamed my money for the failure of our marriage. But he didn't stop there. You name it, my grandfather's legacy and my crass materialism were responsible for it: Vietnam, racism, air pollution. Sidney had conceived the notion that he might have been a great artist without the burden of that money.

Sidney claimed to be above money. Money was something middle-class people, small-minded people, concerned themselves with.

Not that he ever had any trouble spending my money. It paid for his trips to California. It paid for the kids' wacky schools. It made it possible for Sidney to leave me and the children to find God and not have to support any of us. It even ended up paying for that lunch, to which *he'd* invited *me*.

But he hated me for my money. It interfered with his idea of himself as living in a state of virtuous poverty. I was the money-changer in Sidney's temple.

I had always thought that, despite our differences, Sidney and I shared a great deal. But as he talked, I saw this wasn't so.

Here he did me a great kindness. He didn't intend it as a kindness but that, in retrospect, is what it was. For as I listened to him, not only did it seem to me impossible we could ever have been married; I didn't know who Sidney was any more.

When he finished speaking there was dead silence. We sat there, glaring at one another. "Well," I finally said, thinking some levity might improve matters, "have we gotten everything straight?"

Sidney didn't smile. He reached for his mala and swung the locket with the picture of Babadahs back and forth, back and forth. Absentmindedly, he touched several wooden beads with his index finger, as if counting the rosary.

Then he stood up. "Here," he said, scrounging about in his orange overalls pocket. He threw three crumpled dollar bills on the table, not even enough for the tip. Then, before striding out of the restaurant, he leaned across the table, put his face nearly into mine. "You always were a bitch," he said quietly.

IV

COWBOYS AND INDIANS

Have you read *Siddhartha?* Well my father *was* Siddhartha. He had many, many lives. He was one of those extraordinary human beings who are able to turn the coin and leave one life behind and start another.

actress Barbara Carrera

July 1986

"Daddy," i called. The sun had been up only an hour when I came by for Dad at his digs.

I stood in the atrium, surrounded by violets set about in pots on the brick floor. The atrium's as far as you can go and still keep your shoes on.

And I wanted to keep them on. If I went upstairs Dad'd never come down.

At the edge of the bricks were the shoe bins. All those shoes and boots, jumbled together, cozy, like they knew each other, Dad's boots standing a little to the side, the laces tied together.

People think you're un-American if you don't wear shoes indoors. They don't care if you've strolled through a kennel of dog doo, as long as you're wearing shoes. no shoes, no service. The dumbest idea ever.

"Daddy." My voice traveled up through the pine timbers and rattled the big skylight on the top floor where Dad lives. Well, not exactly the top floor; there aren't any floors. Each room hangs off the staircase like a treehouse on its own big branch.

Lotus House is like a lot of buildings on the ranch. They didn't go up with any plan; they just grew. Now *House Beautiful* is doing a story. They sent a whole crew of writers and photographers out to Oregon.

We could use the good publicity. Usually it's "Guru's Disciples in Orgiastic Rites," "Fanatics Paint Oregon Orange."

"Daddy!" I called. I was impatient. After all, this was Enlightenment Day, twenty-seventh anniversary of the day Babadahs dropped His ego forever and discovered He was the reincarnation of Buddha. I was dressed in my new orange gown with the red sequins. I wanted to look great for Babadahs.

That's one of our new songs, composed for this year's celebration: "Looking Great for Babadahs."

> Looking great for Babadahs
> Looking great for Babadahs
> Through his love,
> Life fits me like a glove.
> I'm looking great for Babadahs.

The ashram band's been playing it. Remember that British band, Aluminoid? The lead guy with yellow, curly hair down to his waist and tight black leather pants? Nasty? He's now lead guitar for us. Name's Prem Shanti.

I've been with him lately. Typical Pisces. He sends me little notes with hearts on them and calls me "Luv."

It's been like a party all week, what with fifteen thousand disciples pouring into the ashram for the celebration. They fly into Portland, come over the mountains in Buddhafield buses, and there, at the entrance to the ranch, stretched across the desert road, is this huge banner: WELCOME LOVERS.

I've gone downtown to watch them get off the bus: bushy Africans in orange dashikis, squeaky-clean Japanese, tall sober Swedes. Some with those neat malas they gave out in the early days in India, the beads darker, smaller, rubbed smooth, Babadahs' picture behind beveled glass. "Charter member malas," we call them.

All these fine folks, strutting around in orange. And not just one orange, five hundred—from almost red to ocher to near yellow. It's a regular fashion parade here: tunics, capes, serapes, ponchos, stretch pants with stirrups, jungle pants, jogging suits, Inca hats, leg warmers, cowboy boots, elf boots. This one like Buck Rogers, that one like Wonder Woman or Captain Nemo. Outrageous.

The men with long hair and beards, the women all natural: hair all frizzed out and no bras. Dad says you see more tit here than in *Playboy*.

With all these overseas disciples coming to the celebration, coming home, the atmosphere's been full of juice, electric. If you stood still for a second you could feel it zapping around your ankles.

Never saw so many people so full of love. Everybody hugging. You couldn't walk down Zen Road or the path leading up to Lao Tzu Dining Hall without passing a dozen couples hugging. Some folks hugging so long and still you'd think they were statues.

Lots of us haven't seen each other since India is why. I saw Dodhi yesterday, a lover in India. He lives at the Cologne, Germany, ashram with Ma Yoga Bartee now, but that's okay. We're not into possessions. Everybody is everybody's lover here.

The three of us had a long, long hug on Buddha Road. I felt really together with them.

I mean, what Dodhi and I had still exists somewhere in the universe. It's like physics: Matter can neither be created nor destroyed.

I borrowed a car from the motor pool and took Dodhi and Bartee for a ride out Zen Road as far as we could go. After the paved part — what we call "downtown" — it's dirt for miles. Then it becomes overgrown, with nothing but two rutted tracks and a big hump in the middle.

The old me would have turned around at this point, but I kept going another mile or so. Thank you, Babadahs.

That road is really neat. It isn't going anywhere; just going. There's nothing at the end of it but a wall of weeds.

Dodhi, Bartee, and me got out of the car. There were little mountains as far as you could see, and the ashram owned all of them, it was all ours. We stood in the sage and cornflowers and poppies, with grasshoppers jumping around us, and Dodhi said, "Far out."

The visiting disciples really freak at all the land we've got, a hundred square miles. In India we had four acres; here we need three acres just to store our road graders and earth movers.

"Daddy," I called again.

There was a stir up above. "Hey," someone yelled, "you're wanted below." Whoever said it was way up there, but it sounded like he was next to me.

You hear everything in Lotus House. Dad says it's like living with a tribe of monkeys, each chattering on his own branch. Someone sneezes in that building, everyone knows who.

Dad says he likes it, says privacy is the worst thing about the western world. The American family sucks because everyone is off in their own rooms watching their own TV shows. Nobody relates.

I can cop to that. In high school I knew a girl who had three brothers, so with her mother and father there were six in the family, and they had seven television sets. "So we can watch what we want with no fights," she said. Seven? "In case one's in the repair shop," she said.

I mean, like, gross.

We don't have television, in the ashram, we're too isolated. Isn't that great, to be that isolated?

But even if we did have television it wouldn't belong to anyone in particular. Nobody would say, "This is mine, get out of my face." What we've got here in the ashram is a *real* family; we share everything. Some of us don't even close the door when we tuck One time I wish I had. We were fooling around in Prem Shanti's room, me and him and about eight other people. It started out with a big hug. We were hugging and hugging and nobody wanted to be the first to let go. So then people started kissing and pretty soon it got so elaborate you didn't know whose parts belonged to who. Things were really cooking when Dad and Isabel, his wife, appeared in the doorway. "Far out," they said, and waded right into the pack.

I about shit.

I don't know if Dad knew I was in the room. We've never discussed it. But no way was I staying there with my own father carrying on in the same group. Maybe I'm narrow-minded, but as soon as I could I disconnected myself from a few people and crawled out of the room.

Dad's a free spirit and that's great. But he can be an awful flake sometimes. Like, where was he now? He said he'd meet me down here twenty minutes ago. And even then he acted like he was doing me a big favor, this being Enlightenment Day. Usually Dad doesn't agree to meet anyone anywhere. He says, "If we meet, that's okay, and if we don't, that's okay too." I can dig it—sometimes.

"Daddy," I called once more.

"'Daddy,'" I heard someone mimic me up above. "Hey, 'Daddy,'" the voice repeated, "get your ass downstairs already."

After a while someone was creaking down the stairs. Flight after flight, like they were coming down the Washington Monument that building's so high. They were padding along in their socks, but the steps groaned and the building shook like it was alive.

Nuts, it was Sunshine, this lover Dad sees sometimes. She looked frowzy, like she'd just gotten out of bed. "Dressed already?" she said. "I'd better hurry." She took these beaded American Indian moccasins out of the bin and ran out the door in the direction of Pythagoras House, where she rooms next door to Isabel. Isabel knows all about Sunshine and Dad and thinks it's great.

Isn't jealousy a crock? Thank you, Babadahs.

Now someone else was coming down the stairs. Creak, creak, creak. They were sure taking their time. Then the creaks stopped altogether. I looked up and saw Dad hugging somebody halfway up the house. Nuts. Will you hurry up, Dad?

Dad is champion hugger of the ashram. He walks past Elijah Post Office and hugs everyone in sight. Not like people who do it only with their arms, asses stuck out, making sure their parts don't touch. Dad hugs people so they stay hugged.

Folks in the ashram say, "Run for your lives, here comes Anudaba the Hugger." A lover had a T-shirt made up for Dad at Babadahs Boutique which says in big orange letters on the front, HUGGERMONSTER.

Dad hugs me every time he sees me. I like it mostly, though sometimes I think he takes those corny bumper stickers too seriously, you know, HAVE YOU HUGGED YOUR KID TODAY?

Dad says Babadahs taught him the sense of touch. I can dig it. Though I'd just as soon he didn't talk about how he and Mom never really touched each other. I don't want to hear about that.

Creak, creak, creak. Finally, Dad was continuing down the staircase. He turned the corner at the last landing and I saw he was wearing his orange, martial arts outfit with the magenta sash and carrying his aikido stick. He was going to be part of security today. "Hi, Dad," I said.

Dad sat down on the bottom step and put on his boots. He didn't say anything. Did he have a burn on or what?

We took the path over the little mountains. Nobody was up there, but below you could see disciples coming from all directions, through the canyons and along the river valley. All those orange people moving over the land in the same direction: drops, then rivulets, then waves of orange people. Finally, an ocean of orange people as we got closer to Buddha Hall.

I was feeling really mellow as Dad and I came down from the hills. But as we approached the first disciples, Dad looked at me sideways and said, "Try to remember to call me Anudaba today, okay?"

That's how he is sometimes. Usually, he's an absolute sweety pie but, other times, well . . . .

Still, he was right: nobody calls anyone "Daddy" or "Mommy" in the ashram, not even little kids. People never say "your father" to me; they say "Anudaba."

Usually I remember to call him Anudaba; it isn't as if I want to play kid-parent games.

Mom's part of the problem here. In Griggstown she laid a trip on me when I called Dad "Anudaba." "What's this?" she wanted to know. "'Father,' 'Dad,' is his name, and don't you forget it. If he wants to call himself 'Anudaba' that's his business, but he's your father, and you'll respect your father whether he wants you to or not."

Then she said, "I can't control you when you're not with me. But in this house you will follow the rules of this house."

"Oh, Mother," I said. After all, protesting "Anudaba" is just a way of protesting the whole thing.

Still I always feel a little disloyal to her when I call Dad "Anudaba." To Mom it means she's lost me for sure. She already thinks Dad has cast a spell over me; she calls him Svengali or the Pied Piper. She can't imagine I'd want to be a disciple on my own.

I keep telling her, "Look, Ma, you haven't lost me. When I call Dad 'Anudaba' I'm just doing what all the disciples do."

This doesn't impress Mom. So I send her postcards of the ashram and make a big thing of talking about "Daddy this" and "Daddy that." I don't send her any postcards with Babadahs on them. Just the mountains, Krishna Lake . . . like I'm at summer camp. It's hypocritical, but it keeps things cool with Mom.

Sometimes I wonder why I bother. Do you know what Mom sent *me* the other day? A clipping from the *Trenton Times* with the headline "Local People Members of Indian Cult." There was Mom holding forth about me and Dad. Made me sick. All the kids I went to high school with probably read that thing.

Mom gave the newspaper pictures of Dad and me before we became disciples and pictures Grandma took of us last year in New York. In the old pictures Dad was wearing a cardigan sweater, had a crewcut, was smoking a pipe. I was in a sky blue pinafore and Mary Janes. I liked the new pictures better — our hair so natural and our tans. But people reading the article probably thought we looked like the Manson Family.

The gist of the article was that Dad and me had flipped out. The word "brainwashed" appeared every other line. That's always the big word in the press about Babadahs' disciples: brainwashed.

Mom was quoted as saying she still hoped we would "come to

our senses" one day. I nearly phoned and said I wanted nothing more to do with her. Good thing I showed the clipping to Dad first. He was cool. Looked at the clipping and laughed. "Ignore people when they try to make you crazy," he said.

That's Dad: doesn't let stuff bother him. He's even been sweet about Mom lately. One time I asked him, "Dad, if you could change one thing about your past life, what would it be?"

Well, first he said he wouldn't change anything about his past life; it was perfect just the way it was.

"Sure," I said. That's what Babadahs teaches us. Thank you, Babadahs.

But I pressed him and he said, "I wouldn't have laid so much shit on your mother."

Poor Mom. I do feel sorry for her sometimes. She leads such a narrow life, always hoping things will return to the way they were, always talking about when things were "normal."

Normal? Normal was Mom and Dad yapping at each other round the clock and me and Harry standing around not knowing what to do. So we'd get stoned and try to ignore them. We even took 'ludes a couple of times and went around all rubber-legged for hours.

Normal? I'd get off the school bus in Griggstown and approach the house and you could feel the bad vibes. Hell, you could *see* them: waves, emanations, coming off the house like it was haunted or something.

Normal? Why can't Mom accept things the way they are? Why can't she just let me have my life? Maybe even have her own.

Do you know what I wish Mom would do? Find somebody and fuck her brains out. But she's always saying, "Someone's got to be responsible." Okay, but who elected her?

I mean, Mom's so damn responsible. Years ago, me and Dad were visiting Harry in camp up in Massachusetts, and on the way back we stopped to get some gas and candy. Dad put a quarter in the candy machine inside the gas station office and out came a Mounds bar. We were about to go back to the car when I pulled the lever again—like checking the coin return in a telephone booth, just in case—and out came another Mounds bar. So then I pulled a different lever and out came an Almond Joy. So I pulled another lever and out came a Baby Ruth. So I pulled another lever and out came a Heath bar. So I pulled another lever and out came a Chunky. Outrageous.

Then I went down the line again pulling every lever and got one more each of Mounds, Almond Joy, Baby Ruth, Heath, and Chunky— just about my favorite candy bars when I was a kid. Then I worked the last two levers for a while and got five bags each of Planters Peanuts and Lifesavers.

It was like Las Vegas, only a jackpot every time.

Dad stood there laughing. "Life," he said, raising his hands like a prophet, "is one big candy machine."

Luckily, the gas station guy was busy at the pumps. I got another twenty-five candy bars and me and Dad stuffed them in our pockets. When no more would fit we waddled out to the car. Better haul than I ever got doing Trick-or-Treat and you could be sure there wasn't any cyanide or razor blades.

Dad and me pulled away from that gas station high as kites and laughed all the way back to Griggstown.

But when we got home Mom didn't think it was funny at all. "What about the poor man who runs the gas station?" she wanted to know. "Don't you think you had a responsibility to return the candy and report the defective machine to him?" Good old responsible Mom.

I mean she was right, of course. She's always "right." But can't there be one time in life when candy drops from machines like manna from heaven and you don't have to be a goody-two-shoes about it?

And the funny thing is, now I never eat candy. I mean *sugar,* man. You'd think Mom would have worried about the sugar, not about the guy in the gas station with his candy machine who's no better than a dope pusher and deserved to be ripped off.

Mom pretty well worries about everything. Like, she's always hassling me about the future—what am I going to do if the ashram closes down or Babadahs dies or something?

How do I know? What is life, some big contingency plan? If the ashram ever closes down I'll do what I do then. *This* is what I'm doing now.

Mom came for a weekend visit a few weeks ago. I could tell she didn't want to for herself; she was doing her "duty" as a mother. I tried to get her to change dates to be here now, for the Enlightenment Day Festival, but she made it plain she was visiting me, not the ashram.

She didn't even want to do the "Who Am I?" session I'd scheduled for her. I mean, "Who Am I?" is famous; there's a waiting list, and I had to pull strings to get Mom in it. Swami Dipdo, who runs "Who Am I?", was pissed off when I told him she wouldn't be doing it after all.

I did "Who Am I?" a few months ago and really freaked. What you do is you crawl down a short dark tunnel into this windowless building that's shaped like an igloo.

Inside they shine a light in your eyes and Dipdo comes up to you, sticks his face into yours, and yells "Who Am I?"

He means *you*, not him. Dipdo has his face in yours and he never takes his eyes off you, never blinks. You want to look away but he won't let you; he's absolutely merciless. He grabs your chin every time it droops and pulls it up straight.

"Who am I?" he insists.

"Who am I?" moans a chorus of people behind him in the dark. You can't see them but you know they're back there looking at you.

"I'm Ma Prem Jane," you say.

"Who am I?" Dipdo says fiercely. And the people behind him, droning like the damned, say, "Who am I?"

So you start telling your life, especially the things you've never told anyone. But no matter how personal you get they yell "Who am I?" the moment you stop.

"When I was six years old I stole a game of jacks from the five and dime."

"Who am I?"

"When I was sixteen I played with myself every day, even in the high school girl's room."

"Who am I?"

"I hate you. Get your face out of mine."

"Who am I"

"I hate myself."

"Who am I?"

They keep it up, won't let you off the hook. Dipdo has his face in yours and behind him are all the others. You're so tense and nervous any second you might cry. Even worse, laugh.

Your life peels off in layers like an onion. "I'm rotten inside. Sometimes I have a bad taste in my mouth and I think I have bad breath. My cunt stinks."

"Who am I?"

"What do you want from me?"

"Who am I?"

"Do you know what I did once? Me and another kid, we drowned a cat in Griggstown. We put it into a sack and threw it into the canal."

"Who am I?"

"Leave me alone." Everything was coming apart, my whole life.

"Who am I?"

"Leave me alone," I screamed.

"Who am I?"

I swung, hit Dipdo in the face. Later, I saw he had a red welt on his forehead.

"Who am I?" he said like nothing had happened.

"I'll tell you who I am. At eighteen I got raped. These two guys picked me up hitchhiking, and they drove around and did it to me in the back seat."

"Who am I?"

"Enough! Leave me alone! Leave me ALONE!"

"Who am I?"

"No!"

"Who am I?"

"Who am I? Who am I really? Do you want to know? Do you really want to know how disgusting I can get? Well, get ready for this: when they raped me in the back of that car, I didn't try to stop them. I didn't . . . I didn't . . . I didn't even care."

I fell apart. Hysterical. Misery was bubbling up from so far down I couldn't get it out, couldn't breathe. I was choking. Finally, it surfaced and I cried and cried and cried and cried. I was sobbing and gasping and my whole face was wet.

They weren't asking "Who am I?" anymore. Dipdo had his face in mine, but now it was kind and his arms were around me and everyone in the dark part of the room had come forward and had their arms around me and I loved them all.

Dad was among them, and I went to him, and he put his arms around me and kissed me and quieted me and my sobs began to slow down. "I feel blown away," I whispered to Dad.

"That's what nirvana means in English," he replied.

Pretty soon I was laughing and he was laughing and everyone in the room was laughing. The people in that room were like the best friends I'd ever had.

I felt so clean. Like the past was over and I was really living in the now. Like, I used to be the kind of person who thought so little of herself she could get raped and pretend she didn't care, and now I'm the kind of person who can go up to Prem Shanti and say, "Hey, I like your eyes, want to be with me tonight?" Thank you, Babadahs.

They led me to the back of the room and sat me down among the others, and now I became part of the chorus and a new person crawled into the igloo and "Who Am I?" started all over again.

Anyway, "Who Am I?" was what I wanted to get Mom into when she visited. If anybody needs "Who Am I?", Mom does.

But I couldn't even get her to stay at the ashram. She could have stayed in my room for free or in the Hotel Babadahs. She could have eaten the best vegetarian food in the world. But she preferred to commute from the nearest motel — which is this rundown place in Carson, forty-eight miles away — and eat at Burger King. That's the only restaurant they have in Carson, a Burger King.

I know about that Burger King because one time Prem Shanti and me, we got hold of a car and drove all the way through the desert to Carson for a couple of Whoppers. Nothing tastes better than hamburgers when you're a vegetarian.

We came out of the Burger King feeling a little guilty about it, but Babadahs says, "Better to carry out your fantasy than let it run your life." So we did.

There were some kids on the corner in Carson who kept pointing at our clothes and laughing. One of them yelled at Shanti, "Hey, faggot." And this kid had a big boom box and right at that moment — would you believe? — he was playing an old Aluminoid tape.

I know about Mom's motel too. It's like the motel in *Psycho*. Sinister dog and cat prints on the walls and bedspreads so synthetic you'd want to be real careful about touching them if you just came out of the shower. I know about the motel because that's where they took my friend Shuk when her parents tried to kidnap her.

Prem Shuk's parents visited the ashram, and all day they hassled her about quitting Babadahs and leaving with them. At the end of the day, her father said, "Get in the car," and when she wouldn't, he picked her up like she was a kid or something and threw her in the back seat. Her mother held her down and her father pulled out of the ashram on two wheels.

Lucky thing ashram peace officers spotted them at the front gate and tailed them all the way to the Royal Oaks Motel in Carson. Royal Oaks! There isn't an oak tree within three hundred miles of that motel, and they think *our* names are funny?

Shuk's parents had this guy Bill Johnson waiting in the motel. He's the one on the TV talk shows. Used to be a Moonie and now he makes a living doing what he calls "deprogramming" people.

Deprogramming my ass. Do you know what those deprogrammers do? First they kidnap you, then they beat the shit out of you. Finally, they lock you in a room till you crack. Talk about brainwashing!

Anyway, Shuk hadn't been there ten minutes when she looked out through the venetian blinds and saw the peace officer car in the motel parking lot. She said she had to go to the bathroom. So she went in there, climbed out the window, and *ciao.*

I'll say this for Mom: At least she didn't try to kidnap me when she came for a visit, though it did feel a little like being visited in a sanatorium. Mom sat on a hard chair in my little room and talked in hushed tones like I was sick or something. In the ashram everyone knows everyone else's business, but here were me and Mom in my room, with the door closed and the curtains drawn, whispering together in the dark.

I was so tight I could hardly breathe. Thank Babadahs, occasionally someone would burst into my room and say, "Hey, what's happening, Jane? This your Mom? Far out—" though later Mom said, "Doesn't anyone believe in knocking here?"

"No knocks, no locks," I told her. That's something we say in the ashram. We say a lot of things like that: "No knocks, no locks"; "No shame, no blame." Mom didn't look amused when I told her about "No knocks, no locks," so I skipped "No shame, no blame." And I sure didn't volunteer anything about the bathroom scene here on the ranch which even for me took some getting used to.

In India the johns were co-ed but they had stalls. Here what we've got is these outhouses spread around on the hills, all three- and four-holers. There isn't a one-holer on the ranch or I'd have found it.

The outhouses—"shitters" we call them—have sides and a roof but no front to keep them smelling sweet. Sitting there you might as well be outside. People go by on the trail and say "Hi."

When I first got to the ranch and checked out the outhouses I thought, Oh fuck. How'm I going to handle this? First time I had to go I ran up and down the trail a hundred yards in each direction to see if anyone was coming before I would sit down. That left me not only out of breath but tighter than a drum inside.

I'm sitting there, finally, trying to concentrate, when along the trail comes this neat-looking guy humming "Babadahs Loves Me." Before I can pull up my pants this guy sits down next to me, takes a shit, wipes his ass, shakes my hand, and says, "Hi, I'm Swami David."

I was going to say, "I don't usually do this," but Swami David was already heading back down the trail and I was still sitting there with my knees locked together so tight they hurt like hell the next day.

For a week after that I'd pass David and pretend not to know him. But he asked me to dance one night at the Babadahs Disco and things went on from there. I still get together with him sometimes.

First time I ever met a man in an outhouse. Of course, today, I could shit alongside the whole ashram and it wouldn't mean a thing.

Fart, too. Here in the ashram, people fart loud, often, and without apology. Probably has something to do with all the soy we eat to get our protein. We have soy burgers and soy milk and soy ice cream and soy margarine. You can make anything out of soy, even candy.

That soy is really something. It's healthy, but after dinner a group of us will be sitting around talking or playing cards and every three minutes someone practically rockets off the chair. It's like the movie *Blazing Saddles*.

Folks let out regular trumpet blasts in the ashram. Sometimes, because it's so quiet in the desert, you can hear one over in the next canyon, as if there's a fox hunt going on over there.

With us a fart is a sign of health. Everyone acknowledges it by saying *"Salud."* *Salud*'s like *Gesundheit*. You hear someone fart and you're not even sure who it is but you yell *"Salud."*

The way this came about is one time we were all sitting around in

Buddha Hall, Babadahs up front, and we were in silent meditation. When we're in silent meditation it's so quiet your ears hurt.

Anyway, we're all sitting there looking at Babadahs when suddenly, up front, there's the loudest fart in creation. It sounded like somebody'd blown up. This fart rolled around Buddha Hall and over our heads and echoed off the hills outside, a real Paul Bunyan of a fart.

After its reverberations had quieted and everyone in the hall was trying to forget about it and get on with the meditation, Babadahs began to smile.

The smile started slowly, but it got broader and toothier until, pretty soon, He looked like a donkey up there.

Everyone in the hall was smiling now. Then they started giggling. Finally everyone collapsed in helpless laughter.

Maybe it was Babadahs himself who farted, I don't know. Could have been; it came from his general direction.

When the laughing died down Babadahs started it all over again by saying Salud.

You know, it's reason enough to live at the ashram that we've liberated the fart. The rest of the world goes through life with their cheeks pressed together, terrified they'll let out a loud one in public one day and have to leave town and live somewhere under an assumed name; but with us, farting is just something people do. No shame, no blame. It's no different than eating or sneezing or lovemaking or taking a shower.

Like in the showers: you go in there and there's all these shining bodies. Men and women are scrubbing each other's backs and the soap suds are running down everyone's buns into the common drain. There's nothing perverted about it; it's neat and friendly, one big family. Sometimes I take a shower just to see folks. I even meet up with Dad in the showers sometimes.

I know what everyone in the ashram really looks like. Not what they pretend to look like but what their legs look like, how hairy they are, what kind of asses they have. Dad's got kind of a boney ass.

It's weird out there in the rest of the world where people only know small hunks of each other, as if what people are is these faces that bob along on top of clothes.

Oregonians go bananas over our nudity. Little planes fly low over the ranch with these flaming assholes half hanging out of them trying to get a glimpse of somebody's tits down by Krishna Lake.

One time the newspaper *Oregon Times* did a whole spread on nudity on the ranch. You know: tch, tch, tch. Shit there was even a picture of me. I wouldn't have minded, only they'd put a black bar across my chest and my crotch. Made me look like a whore at a raid in one of those magazines like *Men's Life.*

I wished I could have talked about some of these things with Mom, but she'd have flipped out. She wouldn't even go to the bathroom all the time she was visiting me; held it in. She'd been here a couple of hours when she asked where the toilet was and when I told her about the outhouse scene, she got kind of pale and didn't say anything for a while.

That was okay because Mom and me kept running out of things to say anyway. In the pauses I'd suggest a tour of the ashram, but Mom kept coming up with news of New Jersey, as if I was lonely out here and hungry to know what was going on "back home." She still didn't get it: the ashram was home; being with Babadahs was home.

By the time Mom left Saturday I was completely wired. When she kissed me and drove off towards Carson I ran to Krishna Lake, peeled off my clothes, and jumped in.

Mom was back Sunday right on time. She'd said eleven o'clock and there she was, yes sir, on the button, no rest for the weary. Brought me a bunch of books to read, saying, "I noticed yesterday you had nothing to read in your room. You might as well improve your mind while you're here."

I didn't tell her we don't really read in the ashram. Oh, we read Babadahs and books on Zen and astrology, but we don't want to "improve" our minds; we want to drop them, we want to get them out of the way. And here was Mom bringing me *I'm O.K., You're O.K.* and *Dress For Success.* She apologized that her selection was so meager; the drugstore's the only place to buy books in Carson.

The only book that interested me at all was *I'm O.K., You're O.K.* I'd heard of it. But right away I saw how primitive it was. We learn what that book tells you the first day at the ashram. I'm O.K., you're O.K. is what we *do* here.

I obviously didn't tell Mom this, didn't want to hurt her feelings. But a couple of days later I put the books in the paper recycling bin.

Mom seemed worried about something when she came on Sunday. I pressed her, but she kept shaking me off. Finally she admitted she couldn't decide whether to see Dad or not.

She didn't have anything specific to talk to him about. She thought of it as a courtesy call.

Of course, Anudaba knew she was coming that weekend. He made it clear he was available but not looking for business. "You tell her if she wants to see me I'll be in Jesus Grove," he said. Dad was working with a construction crew there, knocking together platforms and erecting tents for all the disciples expected for Enlightenment Day.

During festival time those of us living on the ranch quit our regular work to take care of the visitors. Like I've been working at Sufi Information Center. That's a good job for me because usually I do personnel; I know everybody.

Dad's normally in publications, but he really grooves on construction work. All he talks about lately is two-by-fours, Phillips head screwdrivers, plumb lines, nails.

Mom kept mulling over whether to see Dad or not. It went on for hours. Yes, no, yes, no. And all that time I could tell she had to pee. She kept shifting from one foot to the other.

Mom was trying to maneuver me into saying that if she saw Dad it would prove she was a good person. No way I was getting sucked into that.

Finally Mom kind of casually said, "I guess I'd best say hello to your father," and we got into her car and drove out to Jesus Grove, fourth canyon into the ranch.

We pulled up and there was Dad, carrying a piece of plywood, sweaty and bare-chested in orange painter's pants, with a big hammer hanging off the loop.

"Hello, Sidney," Mom said, forgetting.

Irritation crossed Dad's face, but he let it slide. "Hello," he said, putting down the lumber.

They stood talking, embarrassed, on their best behavior. I walked down to the river, sat on a rock, pulled the petals off a daisy. Love me, love me not. Love me, love me not. Damned if I was staying up there in all that tension.

After about fifteen minutes Mom called down to me, "Jane, I'm ready to go," and I climbed up the bank and got in her car. Mom and Dad bussed each other on the cheek. Well, at least they'd been civil. Mom drove to the ashram gate and I got out. She was driving the rented car to Portland to catch her plane back to New Jersey. "You will be careful, Jane?" Mom said.

"Sure," I said, but I didn't know about what. I mean, I was staying here; she was leaving. She was the one who needed to be careful. As Mom drove off, I ran up the nearest mountain.

The ranch has hundreds of these sensuous, pointy little mountains, each about three hundred feet high. Hills, really, but I like to call them mountains. You can get up one in a couple of minutes if you run.

I raced to the top and watched mother's rental car wending its way up and out of the valley. It would come around a bend in the road, and then it would go behind a mountain and I couldn't see it. It kept appearing and disappearing, getting smaller and smaller, until it just disappeared for good into the desert somewhere between here and Buffalo.

I kept staring at that spot. Then I gave a "Yip" and, leaning over backwards, spun around three hundred and sixty degrees, watching all those clean little mountains whip by. They make me feel rich. There's so many of them, I could run to the top of any of them and no one would be there. Maybe no one has ever been up there.

Dad got me started going up these mountains. We were walking on Zen Road one day and he said, "Come on," and, before I could respond, he was running up this mountain which came right to the edge of the road.

I followed, none too keen. These mountains are covered with loose shale and are awfully sandy. "Come on" Dad yelled down to me.

"Okay, okay." I tore up the mountain, digging my feet in sideways, my shoes filling with sand.

When I got to the top, out of breath, Dad was calmly waiting for me. "Too bad we don't have wet branches and a blanket so we can send Indian signals," he said. He started waving his arms stiffly like a Navy signalman.

"You're nuts," I smiled at him.

"Yes," he replied. "At last."

We stayed up there a long time, just poking around, not saying much. Dad scratched in the sand with a stick. I lay down at the edge of the mountain, my chin on my arms.

Down below you could see how the ranch was growing. Housing was going up everywhere, the hammering echoing through the canyons. There was a new paved driveway at Babadahs' house with a couple of Rolls-Royces parked on the apron, and you could see the addition they were putting on the side of Lao Tzu Dining Hall two miles away and smell what they were cooking there for supper. I made a bet with myself: broccoli, rice, and soy burgers.

You could see Big Muddy River ambling through the valley and, beyond Gurdjieff Grove, one of the fifty-acre truck farms, a pump sending water from the river up to the farm. The water was coming out of a pipe and slowly spreading over the sand-colored fields, turning them dark brown. An Air Babadahs plane came in over the hills, dipped its wings at us, and settled down on the airstrip alongside the river. I felt peaceful and content.

Dad pulled me to my feet. We stood at the edge, and he grinned, "Opened or closed?"

"You're nuts," I said again.

"Come on," he said, "trust the mountain." That's a thing Babadahs always says. Like, "Trust the universe, trust the mountain."

A moment later we were tearing down the mountain stone-blind, hand in hand, all that sand and shale clattering around us in mini-avalanches, Dad yelling "Hoo, hoo, hoo."

The wind was in our faces and we were totally out of control, feeling the mountain with our feet, doing what they always tell you not to do in school, in summer camp, in the Girl Scouts: "Walk, don't run."

Faster and faster we went as we approached the bottom, slipping and sliding but never falling, until we charged off the mountain into Zen Road and opened our eyes to see all the sand and pebbles and shale we'd kicked up coursing down to land at our feet.

We just stood there, out of breath and laughing. As if we'd pulled off some wonderful caper, won the lottery, robbed a bank. Me and Dad: Butch Cassidy and the Sundance Kid; Bonnie and Clyde.

If you asked me what's the best time I ever had in my life, that was it. Numero uno. Even better than when Dad and me got all those free candy bars.

People back in New Jersey think Dad's an irresponsible shit of a father. Not only does he join a "cult"; pretty soon his daughter's in the cult too. Yeah, well how many of those people have shared their most outrageous times with their own fathers?

Only I would have liked to hang out with Dad a bit after the adventure on the mountain, you know, savored it. But Dad said, "See you around," and went walking off by himself down the road. Don't get me wrong: you talk about something great, you kill it. That's why Dad walked off; he wanted to keep the experience pure.

But Dad can drive me a little crazy with his spontaneity. Every time I want to plan something, he says, "We'll see." Every time I want to look forward to something, he says, "We'll see." Everything with Dad is "We'll see."

Dad lives totally in the Now. "Look," he says, "we could all be dead by next Tuesday. Just smell the flowers."

Sometimes I think Dad is more like Babadahs than Babadahs is, I swear.

They have a special relationship those two. I don't know if I'm imagining this or what, because Babadahs looks at everyone, but every time He drives by and blesses us at noon, there's something extra in the way He looks at Dad.

Babadahs' drive-bys are the big event of the day at the ashram. At 11:45 a whistle blows and everyone quits work and lines up at the side of this dusty road in the middle of nowhere.

I always try to find Dad and stand next to him at the drive-bys. He doesn't look for me; that's not his style. But he's glad to see me.

We stand there and it gets so incredibly quiet it's awesome. All you can hear is the wind in the canyons and the water of Muddy River gurgling through the desert.

At exactly twelve o'clock, miles off, a cloud of dust is kicked up by something. A whirlwind? At first I'm not even sure I see it; I could be hallucinating out here in this sun. But it's real, and it's moving slowly towards us.

Now the energy starts moving up and down the line of disciples. Some folks moan or squeal with delight. Dad makes this big, deep "Ahhhhhh."

Everyone's hands come together in the namaste, everyone's face lights up. Dad's face is so shiny and stretched it looks like it's going to crack.

I know what he's feeling because I'm feeling it too: sheer joy. This is the best there is, the Greatest Show on Planet Earth. That's what Jesus' disciples probably felt, but, of course, he only had twelve.

Oh, I love Babadahs. I love Him, I love Him, I love Him, I love Him. And I love Dad for giving me Babadahs.

If you asked me what's the one thing I absolutely need, what's the one thing I couldn't do without . . . . If you asked me that, I'd answer right off: Babadahs.

Since Babadahs, I hear things, smell things, see things I never could before. I feel like a miracle.

Babadahs passes by now, one gloved hand on the wheel, the other raised in benediction, moving very slowly, looking into every face, especially into Dad's. It's as if Babadahs and Dad have a secret. Or maybe only Babadahs knows about it because one time, after the drive-by, I said to Anudaba, "How come He looks at you like that?" and Dad didn't know what I was talking about. Or, at least, that's what he said.

It's a good thing Babadahs comes by slow, because He's a terrible driver. One time, after He'd passed the whole line of disciples, He turned to wave and went into the ditch. He got out smiling and namasting, and those closest heard Him say, "You see? Not God after all." Twenty disciples pushed the car back onto the road, Babadahs flashed the "V" sign, and He continued on His way like nothing had happened.

Everybody laughed and had a good time. That's the way it is at the ashram.

Another time, after the drive-by, Babadahs crashed into the ashram cement truck on the Buffalo Road. Hardly damaged the Rolls, but the cement truck was in the shop for a week. There was no explanation for it except, well, Babadahs.

These Oregonians out here think it's disgusting that Babadahs has Rolls-Royces. They think religious figures should be all humble and suffering.

Babadahs says, "I'm no crackpot. I didn't become a guru to hang on a cross."

Babadahs believes God never kicked man out of the Garden of Eden. "This *is* the Garden of Eden," He says. "You just don't know it yet."

The Bible-bangers out here in Oregon don't cotton to such remarks. They don't even like New Yorkers, so you can imagine how they feel about "blaspheming" Indian gurus.

A few weeks ago I was in Portland on ashram business—had to get some computer software and supplies—and I walked by a church. In the glass case outside it said the minister was going to preach that coming Sunday on "Babadahs: The Antichrist in Oregon." Shit. If these people want to find the Antichrist they should look in the mirror.

I went in that church and sat for a while, just to get the feel, maybe to flash my orange clothes and mala a little at the choir rehearsing up front, let them know that here was a real live Babadahs disciple, come and get me. They kept eyeing me while they sang "What a Friend I Have in Jesus." I'll bet they do.

They had a painting of the man himself on the wall. Would you believe?—blond with blue eyes, muscular, hanging on the cross with his hairless armpits. Jesus probably looked something like Anwar Sadat, but these people had made him out as the all-American boy, Robert Redford in drag.

The choir members kept eyeing me. I made them so nervous they kept screwing up the song. Finally, the leader of the choir— this little prissy guy— came back where I was sitting and said, "The church isn't open now, young lady. Come back Sunday." I think the "young lady" pissed me off more than anything. When I went outside, he bolted the door behind me.

Everyone in Oregon is on our case. Like the media go crazy over our guns. "Jonestown II," they say. Fuck, what are we supposed to do when someone calls the ranch every day and says, "We're going to kill that Indian son of a bitch."

And it's not just rednecks. All over Oregon they sell T-shirts and bumper stickers with pictures of Babadahs inside orange bullseyes, and there's an organization of prominent citizen types called Keep Oregon Oregon. Every Thursday they fly over the ranch in a little plane and skywrite gross things like, IF WE WANTED ORANGES WE'D LIVE IN CALIFORNIA.

Keep Oregon Oregon says they're into the environment but, would you believe? they drop leaflets on the ranch. Thousands of these leaflets—with a picture of a big orange rat and the words DON'T NEGOTIATE, EXTERMINATE—come wafting down on the mountains and truck farms and into Muddy River. Dad and me joined the crew of volunteers who went out after work to pick them up. Sometimes you still come across one blowing around in the desert

I tell you, there are some bad people out here. It's like a range war, the cattlemen and the sheepherders again. Or, as Dad says, the cowboys and the Indians.

Security is going to be especially tight today, this being Enlightenment Day. It doesn't help any that our big day is July 3rd — gives these bigots one more reason to hate us. While they're getting ready to eat hotdogs and watch the American Legion parade, we're celebrating our Christmas and Easter rolled into one. They don't think that's too patriotic. Even though on the night of the 4th, we shoot off fireworks too, rockets from all the hills at once, it's gorgeous. You'd think that'd make these people happy, but it doesn't. Some people you just can't make happy.

DAD AND I had arrived at Buddha Hall. Disciples swirled around us, filing slowly in, everybody full of juice like they were going to a rock concert or something.

Dad put his aikido stick in a rack on the side of the hall. For weeks he's attended martial arts classes after work and is so fast with the stick now he can hit a fly on the wing. "Not even kill him," he says. "Just nick his left ball."

Dad never was good at sports as a kid. Had colds and allergies all the time. Now look at him: carpenter, bodyguard, macho man.

Buddha Hall looked special. It had been scrubbed super clean, and as Dad and I entered, all that orange against the glass walls was dazzling.

Up front Prem Shanti and the commune band were playing; the place was rocking out. Man, we just have the most awesome times.

That's why I became a disciple, the good times. I was grim before. Lousy at everything except my school work, and so nervous I shook. I was, well, like Mom.

I went to Sarah Lawrence one semester. Mom said it would give me confidence. She must have been kidding. After one semester in that tight-assed place, I was ready for the loony bin. My skin broke out all over my body — not on my face and hands, but everywhere else, like I had the syph. You could look at me and never know that from my collar to my shoes I was pimples. Really gross. I'd go to the infirmary and the dermatologist would go, "Hmmmmm." He'd test me for allergies and finally said, "Don't drink tomato juice." Wow. Great.

After that, my ovaries got infected. My stomach swelled up like a balloon and it hurt so much I couldn't walk. Now I probably can't have children.

Which is okay, I guess. Kids don't leave you much time to become enlightened.

I'm a little like a nun. Nuns don't have kids; they're married to Jesus. I'm married to Babadahs, but I fuck anybody I want.

When I got to India, Babadahs took care of all my health problems. I haven't been sick once since I became a disciple — except for the intestinal thing everyone gets in India. I've been high all the time, stoned on Babadahs.

Before I became a disciple I didn't even know how to breathe. I'd take short, shallow breaths, like I was rationing the air. I learned how to breathe doing the *Om* — which is what we were doing now in Buddha Hall.

I love the *Om*. This sound comes from deep inside you, starting in your toes and moving up through your organs until you're tingling all over — back, fingers, cheeks. You're freaked on air.

Dad says the *Om* is "celestial music." It sounds like it's coming out of Tibet or from the center of the earth. Like the earth is groaning with pleasure.

And the great thing is that the *Om* isn't just inside you. It's in everyone around you. I peeked at Dad, a little guilty because you shouldn't be looking around. Yep, Dad was stoned too, blissed out on the vibrations.

The floor and the glass roof were vibrating. It felt like Buddha Hall wasn't anchored, was starting to move. Om.

Buddha Hall was a space ship in countdown: 10 . . . 9 . . . 8 . . . . When we hit zero the whole place was going to lift off the ground, slowly at first, but then gaining speed, so that, pretty soon we'd be rocketing towards heaven, all my favorite people in the world, together in our own Yellow — well, Orange — Submarine.

Sometimes I can feel the *Om* so deep inside me, I swear my uterus contracts. It's like when I'm getting my period, only it's nice.

It's almost like a vibrator or something coming up from the floor against my pussy. My friend Prabodhi says she had an orgasm one time when we were doing the Om.

I know what she means, I haven't had one doing the Om, but I've come close.

What mostly happens to me doing the Om is, I flash to past lives. Like in the fifteenth century my name was Abigail and I was a witch. At least, that's what they said about me when they burned me at the stake. I'm not making this up; I've felt the flames. Right there, doing the Om, I felt them and the next day I had these weird marks on my body.

In the eleventh century I died in infancy. Typhus. My name would have been John.

Before John, I was some kind of animal, a cat in Middle Egypt. Well, I'm not sure about the cat, but it was Egypt.

It freaks me out experiencing these past lives, so I always look forward to the Om. Imagine the poor suckers who only know about their present lives!

The Om is a powerful thing. They say that people who *Om* regularly are going to live longer. Doing the Om slows everything down—your breathing, your heartbeat, your blood pressure.

People who Om eat less; they don't wear their bodies out so quickly. Their body is like one of those cars old ladies drive that are twenty or thirty years old with only 18,000 miles on them and the paint like new.

Dad's like that. In pictures of him ten years ago he's so serious he looks ten years older than he does now. Today he looks like a kid.

Maybe we're creating a new race of humans out here, like those people up in the Andes in Peru who eat clay, turn green, and live to be a hundred and fifty. Or like that old movie where the people lived in a tropical valley in the middle of the Himalayas called Shangri-la. Outside it was freezing cold, and if you went out there you crumbled into dust, but inside Shangri-la it was paradise and you lived almost forever. Maybe that's what we're building here, Shangri-la.

But what do people outside think of us? "Bunch of crazy cultists."

What can I tell you? Either you've looked into Babadahs' eyes or you haven't. If you haven't, then you see what goes on here through the window of your own dumb life and the lies they teach you in Sunday school. Everybody says, "Look at those Orange People, smiling like crazies." As if we have to apologize for smiling. Ever notice people in the New York subways? People in elevators? People in church? A little crazy smiling would do those people some good.

If this is a cult and I'm brainwashed, well, fuck, this is a cult and I'm brainwashed. I'd rather be happy and brainwashed than a sad asshole who goes around pointing her finger at other folks and saying they're brainwashed.

The *Om* was still going but slowly dying out around the hall. We were letting go of the *Om* now and sinking into silent meditation.

I like silent meditation almost as much as the *Om*. It's great to be together with all these people in beautiful orange, and everyone's paying attention, everyone's worshipping existence. That's what Babadahs teaches: to worship existence. Not Jesus or Mohammed or even Babadahs Himself. "If you must worship someone, worship yourself," Babadahs says. Thank you, Babadahs.

We were silent a long time, listening to our breathing, feeling our heartbeats. Outside you could hear nature: Big Muddy River drifting by; a bird flapping up into the rocks. Babadahs says, "Learn to be a rock. After you have learned to be a rock you can learn to be a flower. Then you can learn to be a bird. Finally, someday, you might be ready to be a person." The trouble with most of us, Babadahs says, is that we don't even know how to be a rock and we're trying to be people. Thank you, Babadahs.

Pretty soon we were coming out of the silent meditation. Folks began yawning and stretching, whispering, giggling. The energy was going up.

Shanti and the band broke into "Love to Love Your Love," another of the songs composed by the band. "Love to Love Your Love" is one of my favorites.

> Love to love your love
> Babadahs taught me how
> Now I see
> How my life can be
> Love to love your love.

Everybody was getting to their feet to dance and the place was jumping again. Pure juice. Everyone digging themselves and everybody else.

Shanti was at the microphone. "Hello lovers," he shouted. "Hello lovers," we roared back.

Man, we've got a lot of disciples now. I know, because I'm the one who keeps track of them. We're adding seven hundred a week. I get telexes with the information from branch ashrams around the world. Every name I put into the computer, it's like ringing up a sale.

Of course, we also lose some—but only about twelve a week. I'm always sad editing somebody out of the computer. *Blip*, they're gone. I feel like I just killed somebody. I kind of hope they'll reappear in the next printout . But twelve losses, seven hundred gains? Can't do much better than that.

We're growing so fast now, the whole world could go orange. And I don't mean in the next century—now while Babadahs is in His present body.

We're growing so fast they gave me an assistant, Prem Moses. Get this: Prem Moses is fifty-eight; used to be a television producer for NBC in New York by the name of Robert Carter; chucked all that bullshit for Babadahs. And now he assists a twenty-two-year-old girl with only one semester of college. That's the way it goes here.

Prem Moses likes to go around with a flower behind his ear. He's cute. One time, instead of a soy coffee break (real coffee's more addictive than heroin, believe me), me and Prem Moses did it on the floor over by the filing cabinets. We were hugging and, well, you know . . . . Nothing serious. Just a friendly fuck.

Let me tell you: these older guys are regular billy goats. But afterwards, when we got back to our screens, Prem Moses was sleepy and kept making mistakes. I had to chew him out. "No more hanky-panky with the boss," I told him.

Except for that one time, me and Prem Moses work like crazy. "Work as if you're saving the world," Babadahs says, and we do.

We've got the Xenon 1085 at the ashram, state of the art. Babadahs has no hangups about technology versus nature. He says technology *is* nature.

I can access a disciple in ten seconds on the 1085. Say we need a

Swahili-speaking African who can do carpentry and is in the States right now. In ten seconds I've accessed the dude on the screen and two seconds later the Xenon is dialing him on the phone. Most days I can hardly wait to get to work in the morning. They've got outrageous cereal over at Lao Tzu—rolled oats and wheat and coconut and hazel nuts and almonds and raisins. They make it fresh every day. But usually I skip breakfast to get as much done as possible before the noon drive-by. Then I pig out at lunch. That's the great thing about being a veggie: it hardly matters how much you eat.

Before I came to the ranch I had to survive for five weeks on the garbage they fed me at this hotel in Portland. I nearly died. I was in Portland to study computers for four weeks at the university. Then I got checked out for a week on the Xenon.

Now there's three thousand of us living at headquarters, but when I arrived there were less than a hundred and things were primitive. Babadahs Himself had only been at the ranch six weeks.

The way He got here is He left India on a chartered Flying Tigers jet, with a Rolls-Royce crated up inside. Came to America because, well, this is the land of the free and the home of the brave, isn't it? Flew straight to Portland; Ma Anand Devora had found this huge spread of land for sale, cheap, in eastern Oregon.

When people think of Oregon they picture rain and big trees, but east of the Cascades Oregon's a desert. Perfect for us. Nobody wanted it; nobody would bug us here.

Babadahs and Devora and Swami Nirvana, who handles finances, and Ma Mukdha, who used to be in real estate in Los Angeles, got into the Rolls-Royce at Portland airport and headed east. Everything was green until they were coming down off the slopes of Mount Hood. There was this line across the land and after that everything was brown and gritty.

Swami Nirvana was behind the wheel because Babadahs has no license. (Can you imagine them making Babadahs take a driving test? Like checking out Jesus on his burro.) But when they got to Buffalo, where the highway ends, Babadahs wanted to drive. So they got out of the car to change places.

Buffalo looks like the Twilight Zone. It has only forty people, and none of them were in the street. The only thing moving was this windmill pumping water at the end of Main Street, which is actually the only street in Buffalo.

After a while screen doors squeaked open and some folks came out into the dusty street. They looked at the gleaming, white Rolls-Royce and at Babadahs and at the others as if, Holy Shit, the Martians have landed.

A kid giggled.

"Quiet," his mother snapped.

"But Ma," the kid said, pointing at Babadahs with his long robe, his curlicued slippers, his jewel-encrusted hat, and his long white beard, "it's Santa Claus."

Babadahs smiled and namasted, but the people shrank back. Babadahs *is* Santa Claus, only those people in Buffalo were too dumb to recognize Him. These were God-fearing Christians here.

"Might it be possible," Babadahs asked, "to purchase a cup of tea?"

Tea? That was a joke. We're talking about a town where some people have never had tea in their lives. Tea's for foreigners and weirdos.

Babadahs smiled and namasted again. "A little water, then?"

These people took their children by the hand, backed up inside their houses, and slammed the doors. It got real quiet again. Not a sign of anyone except a couple of kids peeking through the curtains. Some tumbleweed blew in from the desert and down Main Street.

Babadahs and the others got into the car and picked up the dirt track that leads out of town towards the Big Muddy Ranch. It's twenty miles of the most nothing road in America, washboard and sand; so sandy, the Rolls traveled sideways as much as forward. And with Babadahs at the wheel, it was a wonder it stayed on the road at all.

As you come out of Buffalo the land rises and the hills begin. There are no markers so you have to keep your eyes on the odometer if you want to know where you are. Ten miles, twelve, fifteen. At seventeen miles, you come over the highest of the hills, and down below is the valley of the Big Muddy.

They got out of the car and Babadahs said, "Looks good."

Later, some disciples claimed Babadahs had said, "This is the place," same as what Brigham Young said when the Mormons came to the lip of the Wasatch Mountains in Utah and looked down into the valley of the Great Salt Lake.

But all Babadahs said was, "Looks good." He likes to keep things light. "Light," He says "is enlightened."

Three days later, Nirvana, who used to be on Wall Street, paid seven million dollars cash for the ranch, a million and a half of it his own; and three days after that mobile homes were being trucked in over the mountains and Oregon Electric was pounding in telephone poles like wooden pegs all the way from Buffalo to Rancho Babadahs.

When I got to the ranch a few weeks later, there were still so few of us I got a personal greeting from Babadahs. He was living in a mobile home then, but the place glowed. Babadahs sat there in His egoless state, looking like pure love. I kneeled at His feet.

He didn't say anything for a while, just looked at me with those giant brown orbs. Finally, reaching over to pat my head, He said "So you're the young woman who's going to keep track of us?"

I nodded. Never felt so proud in my life.

"And how is Anudaba?" Amazing. Half a million disciples and He remembers Dad's name.

"Dying to come out here," I replied.

"Tell him he doesn't have to die to come out here," Babadahs said.

That night I phoned Dad in New Brunswick. We had only one phone line then, and I had to wait half the evening to use it, but I finally got through to Dad at George Smith's apartment. I'd called collect, and that might have been why Dad came on sounding extra glum. He was stone-broke, and here I was bankrupting him altogether.

But when I told him what Babadahs had said he freaked. "What did He say? What's that now?" What made it difficult was that Dad could hear me, but I could hardly hear him. Every time I spoke my own voice echoed so long I couldn't hear the beginnings of Dad's sentences. "What's that He said? What did He mean exactly by 'Tell him he doesn't have to die to come out here?' Does He want me out there?"

"I don't know," I shouted. "He sounded like it."

Dad was disintegrating on the other end of the line, unsure whether he would be coming out here soon or Babadahs meant nothing particular by the remark, was just being funny.

Anyway, a month later Dad was here. By this time we had

enough people so we weren't just a ranch; we were Babadahspuram, which means City of Babadahs.

We even had a zip code. Babadahspuram, Oregon 96532.

Folks in Buffalo tried to stop it. They sent a petition to the Postmaster General in Washington demanding our town be named after some dead local rancher who had been the first county chairman of United Way. Naming it after someone who was not only alive but a heathen Indian pissed them off.

A woman in Carson wrote to the newspaper: "It's like the Communists. first they want a zip code. Then they want something else. Next thing you know we're all speaking Hindu."

When Ma Anand Devora called Dad to tell him to come she let me listen in on the extension. "Far freaking out," Dad yelled. I never heard him so happy.

He arrived the next day and went right to work, sixteen hours a day, on *Babadahs* magazine. He wanted to get out an issue each month—show the world that Babadahs—that the ashram—was alive and well in Oregon.

Dad started to look outrageously healthy out here. I'd see him walking around in high, lace-up boots, an orange mackinaw, orange painter's pants, his face as ruddy as his clothes.

He liked it a lot better here than in India. India was, well, India. Out here, Dad said, "You're a regular shitkicker."

Dad liked that the building where he works in publications has a good American name, Thoreau Temple. Dad used to teach Thoreau. He'd go around saying, "Thoreau Temple. Dig it."

"Temples" is what we call the places where we work. That's because we don't work, actually, we worship. "Work," Babadahs says, "is doing what you don't want to do."

I could worship three hundred sixty-five days a year without a day off and be perfectly happy. Though it's fun, too, when one of our celebration days comes along.

There are four altogether, one for each season: Babadahs' Birthday, Guru Day, Mahpakatana Day—when we celebrate all disciples who have moved on to new bodily forms—and today, Enlightenment Day.

Of course, Enlightenment Day isn't just a celebration, I thought, as Dad and me and everybody else began filing out of Buddha Hall into the sunshine. It's the biggest day in the year; it's *the* celebration.

While we'd been in Buddha Hall, the crew from Lao Tzu Temple had been setting up a feast outside: a giant vegetarian brunch, what had to be the largest salad bar in the world, all of it grown by us. People think vegetarians are martyrs. Fuck, we eat like kings and queens, and there isn't one fat person here. We eat low down on the food chain, vegetables and roots and nuts and fruits—stuff that's easy to digest and doesn't give you cancer. Vegetables are where it's at; meat is poison. Just smell the sweat of people who eat meat. Phew! People smell good in Babadahspuram—and we don't use deodorants or any of that garbage. In Portland, when I ride the bus, I stick my head out the window or I gag. All those "civilized" people, scrubbed clean and feeling superior to me in my weird garb, but oozing shit from every pore.

I'll tell you something: I draw the line somewhere. I don't care about a person's age, race, religion, or who or what they have sex with. But meat-eaters? Forget it.

People assume vegetarians have a problem killing animals. That's true of some, and I can dig it, as long as they don't go around wearing leather shoes and belts anyway. At the ashram, killing isn't the thing. We just want to be healthy and not stink.

We also want to feed people not cows. Dad says it takes six acres of grass to feed one cow, and we grow enough food on six acres to feed fifty people. Like everybody's worrying about the starving Ethiopians. Fuck, if everybody was a vegetarian, the population of the globe could triple—fifteen billion people—before anybody'd go hungry.

The way our chalky hillsides were now covered with orange disciples it looked like there already were fifteen billion people and they were all here, eating their veggies. Then, as folks finished eating, outrageous things started happening. Jugglers. Mime. Swami Majareshi walking a tightrope he'd stretched between two mountains. Our own carnival.

And then, over the mountains, from where I don't know, came a big hot air balloon, with BABADAHS EXPRESS written on it in orange letters.

The balloon was the signal for the drive-by at Zen and Buddha Road crossing, where Babadahs was coming at noon to bless us. We fanned out along a mile of Zen Road, five or six deep, the glass of our mala lockets twinkling in the sun, everybody joking and clowning. There were so many of us I couldn't see the end of the line. Things got quiet. It was as if someone said "Shhhlıh" and the word passed along like a breeze through a wheat field. Everyone's hands came together in the namaste.

We stared down Buddha Road, where it curved behind the mountains. There was a stir in the desert way off, a bit of dust. My heartbeat picked up, my breathing. It was like my birthday, and coming towards me through the heat and dust was all the ice cream I could eat.

How can I tell you what it's like? How does one describe a holy man? "Babadahs is a great poem," Dad once said to me. "He doesn't mean anything. He just is."

And now He was coming.

The dust speck had become a small cloud now, moving over the desert, miles down Buddha Road.

Then the dust cloud separated out into three clouds, probably a scout car for security up front, Babadahs in a Rolls-Royce, and another scout car bringing up the rear. My heart started pounding.

The first khaki scout car rounded the bend and came towards us, looking like it was straight out of Africa—dusty, camouflaged, its spare tire fastened to the hood with a leather strap. Inside were four peace officers, two facing forward, two backward. They held their rifles away from their bodies so as not to tangle them in their malas.

Then Babadahs' Rolls-Royce came around the bend, huge and gorgeous in all that dust. Great big creamy whitewalls, you could almost eat that automobile. Which one was it today, the silver? the blue? the maroon with the white top? Babadahs never drives the same one two days in a row. Gives us a treat.

Someone was riding on the roof of the Rolls. It was Prem Sambodhi in a leather cockpit strapped to the roof, an Uzi cradled in his arms. I saw Dad and the other extra security people peel off from the crowd and surround the Rolls.

I knew how proud Dad was, protecting Babadahs. He'd often said he would give his life for Him without blinking an eye. He meant it too.

The Rolls started on its circuit past the disciples. Somebody put daisies on the hood and, as Babadahs continued along, other disciples put on gladioluses, roses, zinnias. Pretty soon the Rolls' hood was so covered with flowers Babadahs couldn't see out. He stopped the car so they could take off the flowers.

Babadahs continued on, but right away they started covering the car with flowers again. Babadahs stopped every hundred yards so the flowers could be removed. Everyone laughed. And now that Babadahs was close I could see that He was laughing too in His unearthly way behind the tinted windshield.

Dad was also laughing, as he walked beside the right front bumper, his aikido stick poised. Laughing, but he didn't take his eyes off the crowd.

Now the Rolls-Royce was pulling alongside me. Babadahs inside, one gloved hand raised, blessing us, the other on the wheel; and alongside Babadahs, Dad. I looked from Babadahs to Dad, from Dad to Babadahs.

The Rolls moved on, and the second scout car came along. The disciples were all falling in behind it down the road.

We walked behind the cortege chanting and throwing rose petals into the air; so many of us we were like a tribe moving over the desert. The Children of Israel following Moses. Our own Hollywood movie with a cast of thousands.

How beautiful everyone's face was. I wanted to kiss each one. I *did* kiss a lot of them.

Somewhere up front the band began to play. Actually, there were many bands. Anyone with an instrument — guitars, tambourines, bongo drums, maracas, flutes, harmonicas — was banging away on it as we walked in the dusty road. Some folks were even humming on combs or knocking rocks together. It was wonderful. It felt — well, like suddenly the world had a real chance.

The band began to play their new song, "Babadahs Is the World," and we shouted to the hills:

Babadahs is the world
Babadahs is the future
Babadahs is the world
For Babadahs is love.

Babadahs is the world
Babadahs is fulfillment
Babadahs is the world
And Babadahs is joy.

Babadahs is the world
Babadahs is nature
Babadahs is the world
Babadahs is God's pleasure.

Babadahs is the world
Babadahs is the world
Babadahs is the world
And Babadahs is the world.

The Rolls and scout cars reached the end of the long line of disciples. Babadahs got out and mounted a wooden platform, like a lifeguard stand, which had been erected by the side of the road. Tonight He would be addressing all of us in Buddha Hall, but now He just stood there smiling, namasting to the East, to the West, to the North and to the South. Then He descended the few steps and got back into the Rolls.

Prem Sambodhi got off his perch on the car's roof, and Dad and the other security people gently pushed back the crowd. When everyone was clear of the cars, the first scout car leaped forward and the Rolls and second scout car followed. The scout cars tried to stay as close to Babadahs as possible without crashing into Him.

We ran down the road after the cars. We knew we couldn't catch up with Babadahs but it was fun to try. I loved running full out that way with everyone. There were thousands of us, laughing and raising a great cloud of dust.

Babadahs was already a quarter mile ahead of us, about to turn up the road into Bal Shem Tov Canyon, when suddenly, from the mountain in front of Him, a tiny puff of smoke arose. There was a flash of flame, and Babadahs' Rolls-Royce leaped into the air and crashed onto its side, as the sound of the explosion finally reached us.

Everyone stopped dead.

Then we were running towards the Rolls. Prem Sambodhi cut left and up the first mountain, firing the Uzi at something. The peace officers piled out of the scout cars and were running up the hillside.

Later, we learned that all they found up there was a bazooka, still hot. Also two pup tents and litter—but the bushwhackers were gone. On the other side of the mountain was an ancient dirt track with the dust still hanging in the air from the departing four-wheel-drive vehicle they had come in with the night before.

When the first disciples reached the Rolls, the wheels on the left side were still turning and there was a fire in the motor. Babadahs had fallen out and the automobile had almost rolled on top of Him. They dragged Him away just before the Rolls exploded.

They laid Babadahs down in the sage at the side of the road, and Swami Swapdo, our doctor, examined Him.

There was nothing to do. His skull was smashed. The light slowly went out in those enormous brown eyes.

But before He died, Babadahs did one thing. I didn't see it because there were too many disciples in front of me. But those up front said He raised His hand and made some kind of sign. It sounds crazy, but most thought he made the sign of the cross.

Babadahs always said the cross was a symbol of cruelty not love. So what did He mean? Could He have been comparing himself to Jesus, saying we're all Jesuses, we're all martyrs? I don't know. Nobody in the ashram knows.

Some folks insisted Babadahs hadn't made the sign of the cross. It was some other sign. Or maybe He had just raised His hand involuntarily; it didn't mean anything.

Ma Anand Devora took charge of the funeral. She said we should come back to Buddha Hall five hours later. Meanwhile, disciples walked around like zombies. You could hear the wailing in every canyon.

I went to Lotus House looking for Dad, hoping we might just hug each other. He was gone, but he had been there. His aikido stick lay on the bed, broken in two.

An hour before the funeral, everyone began to gather outside Buddha Hall where earlier we had been so happy. We sat on the ground. At six, Babadahs' body was carried to the huge funeral pyre. There were no flowers around it; Babadahs' body was flower enough.

No words were said. There was nothing to say. The greatest being on earth had been murdered.

We watched as the flames traveled up the high stack of wood. Sat there not even able to cry, dead as Babadahs' body.

But where was Dad?

As the flames moved higher, the band began to play "Love to Love Your Love," and a few disciples sang, mournfully, like a dirge. I didn't want to sing. Even though Babadahs always said, "Celebrate everything. Especially death."

"Love to love your love
Babadahs taught me how
Now I see
How my life can be
Love to love your love."

Ma Anand Devora shouted into the microphone: "Dance!"

We struggled to our feet and tried to move our bodies. At first it was impossible; we were so numb. But moving primed the pump; the blood began to circulate a little.

"Dance! Sing!" Ma Anand Devora commanded. The band picked up the rhythm. The pace kept increasing as the flames circled Babadahs' body.

The only thing between us and absolute madness was the music and the dancing. "Dance! Sing!" Devora kept yelling.

And now it began to happen. Tears. Laughter. For a moment you could imagine you were dancing for fun around a giant bonfire.

But where was Dad? I wanted to be sharing this with him: the horror and the joy shining through the flames. Where was he?

Now the entire pyre was aflame and you couldn't see Babadahs' body anymore. The pace of the dancing and singing picked up still more.

"Dance! sing!" Devora kept yelling, but it wasn't necessary. We had to do something, so we danced

We danced and sang for hours. Danced and sang as the pyre burned down and there were only glowing coals. Danced and sang as Devora and Nirvana and some of the other leaders crept in among the embers to find Babadahs' ashes and put them in an urn.

Danced and sang even though it was dark and there was no longer any light from the fire. Danced and sang almost all night, like crazy people who weren't going to stop dancing because, if we did, we would die.

And still no Dad.

Finally, in twos and then tens and then hundreds we staggered away from Buddha Hall to try to sleep. Hoping somehow that when we awoke this would all be a dream.

At my house someone was standing in the shadows. I thought it might be Shanti. Tired and sick as I was I thought, "Why not? What better time?"

But it was Dad standing there in the shadows. I went up to him hoping Anudaba, the great hugger, would put his arms around me. But he was weird. He just stood there, his arms at his side, not really looking at me, not saying anything. I put my arms around him. "Daddy," I said, rubbing his back, but he was like a stone.

"Daddy!" I said sharply, hoping to snap him out of it, and again, "Daddy!" But he just stood there, that strange look on his face, a look that somehow went even beyond the excruciating grief the rest of us were experiencing.

"Come inside, Daddy," I said to him. I thought maybe I could put him to sleep in my bed and then go sleep in his room in Lotus House. "Please, Daddy," I said.

But Dad just stood there. And then, abruptly, he turned and walked off into the darkness.

V

SIDNEY FINDS A TRADE

The portent that was seen last night?—a great red letter in the sky—the letter "A" which we interpret to stand for "Angel."

Nathaniel Hawthorne
The Scarlet Letter

September 1986

I DIDN'T KNOW what to expect. The telegram just said: COME. I phoned, but I couldn't get through to Sidney. "He's expecting you," was all I was told.

I figured Sidney needed me and I was glad. It had been a long time since he'd needed me.

Then a first-class plane ticket arrived. First class. I'd never flown first class in my life. I phoned Elaine and told her about it. "Be careful," she said.

I came down the ramp in Portland and all these orange people were waiting. "Mrs. Kantor?" One by one, they hugged me. Hard. As if we'd known each other forever.

One of the orange people went to get my bag, and the others escorted me to a small orange jet parked a hundred yards away, AIR BABADAHS ONE painted on its side in red.

Ten minutes later I was up in the air again, in a private compartment, the orange people somewhere up front piloting the plane.

What a trip. I sat alone in a great swivel chair. Beautiful Indian fabrics were draped over everything, and sitar music drowned out the motors. There were little cakes to eat and something to drink called "Babadahs nectar." Still, I felt apprehensive, like I was being kidnapped or something.

We were flying alongside Mount Hood now. It was huge and snow-covered and spread out over the landscape in every direction. The newspapers said Babadahs' assassins had disappeared into the woods on the lower slopes. I looked down, trying to spot somebody.

So far, the police have caught one man, an ex-Marine they think is a member of the Ku Klux Klan. They're looking for three or four others, including the leader, a preacher. He's got a congregation in Eugene who call themselves The Church of Christ Crucified, Risen, and Come Again. They showed them on television speaking in tongues and parading around with poisonous snakes.

When Babadahs was killed, it was on television every day for a week. But I was too worried about Sidney and Jane to think about Babadahs. I wondered what they would do with their lives, especially Sidney. He couldn't go back to the university. And the newspapers said that, with Babadahs dead, the ashram was going to break up. When I saw Sidney I would invite him to live with me until he got his bearings.

The plane passed the eastern slopes of Mount Hood and, right away, the green gave way to desert and the plane started down. We circled over brown hills, and then I saw buildings below and in the middle of them what looked like a huge orange stain. The plane came in over a river which ran between the hills and set down on a dirt strip in the valley.

When it came to a stop I looked out the window and saw that the orange stain was Orange People, thousands of them, moving towards the plane. As I stuck my head out the door a great shout went up. "Mrs. Kantor," they all cheered, and a band on a flatbed truck struck up "Hava Nagila." That was nice of them.

At the foot of the stairs was an orange carpet. Everyone thronged around me, throwing rose petals into the dusty air. They wanted to touch me—my cheek, my hand.

I recognized some of the folks from India, including that German lady who wrestled with me and kept calling me "Adele." She knelt and kissed the hem of my dress. These people sure knew how to welcome a person.

The crowd parted and Jane came forward, radiant. "Grandma," she said.

Jane led me through the crowd to where a Rolls-Royce purred, a Swami at the wheel. I got in back and Jane followed me inside. It was big as a ship's stateroom in there: polished wood and brass, a bar, a television set. "What's going on, Jane?" I asked.

But Jane just smiled.

The Rolls-Royce moved slowly up the hill, the whole mob following—singing, clapping hands, dancing. The driver talked from time to time into a microphone: "Dove 1 to Dharma House; Dove 1 to Dharma House."

Ahead was a large grove of trees, surrounded by a high fence—"electric," Jane said. At the corners, guard towers poked up through the trees, and at the entrance to the compound two orange people, a man and a woman, cradled Uzis in their arms.

The guards opened the gate, and the Rolls-Royce was driven into a lush garden where fountains splashed among the flowers. A large stone and glass house was set into the rocky hillside. Jane opened a door and said, "Go right in."

"Jane?" I said, hesitating, but Jane just smiled again.

I walked down a long cool corridor. It was quiet except for the whisper of the air conditioning. Along the corridor were alcoves with tropical plants, rock gardens, goldfish in pools.

At the end of the room, seated on a throne like the Wizard of Oz, wearing a long white robe, was Sidney.

At least I thought it was Sidney. He looked like Sidney, but a Sidney who had aged immeasurably, who seemed as old as Babadahs.

Then there was this look on his face. I know my own son, and I can tell you: Sidney never looked like that in his life. He looked like he'd been invaded by the body snatchers; no one was home inside.

I stood there awkwardly, with Sidney looking blankly at me. Well, not at me exactly, more like through me. I wasn't sure he saw me or recognized me.

Finally, Sidney motioned me to sit on the floor in front of him. You'd have thought, since he was occupying the only seat in the room, he'd have gotten up and offered it to me. Strangers do on the bus, couldn't my own son? That's the trouble with these fancy new religions: they forget the simple things like, "Honor thy father and mother."

"Sidney," I whispered. In that place and with that look on his face, you whispered.

Sidney didn't answer. Maybe I was using the wrong name. "Anudaba," I said correcting myself. Later, I learned you didn't call Sidney "Anudaba" anymore either.

I'm thick. It wasn't till then I realized there was something funny here. Could it be? Sidney had become the new guru of the Orange People. They had chosen my Sidney.

This explained my welcome in Portland and at the ashram. Like it or not, I was now Queen Mother of the Orange People.

Sidney's new name was Babadahs Anudaba, Lord God Blessed Slave, for short, Babadahs II, like a pharaoh. Considering he didn't move a muscle, he could have been a mummy for all I knew.

I sat there a full hour with Sidney. He didn't say a word, didn't acknowledge my presence. I guess I was supposed to be grateful for this private audience with the great Babadahs II, his being so important and busy and all, but I could have used a little conversation. Anything. If he'd asked, "How was the trip?" or "How're the

New York Mets doing?" I'd have been satisfied. But Sidney didn't even blink.

Then, abruptly, he got up and strode out of the room. One moment he was there, the next gone. I thought maybe he had gone to the bathroom or something, assuming gurus go, but when he didn't return in fifteen minutes, I retreated down that long corridor and out of the house.

Jane was waiting with the Rolls-Royce. And beyond the compound some of the Orange People were still there. As the Rolls came out the gate they fell to their knees. The mother of the great guru herself, fresh from His presence. Look, I wanted to tell them, even if Sidney has become Jesus Christ, I am not the Virgin Mary.

I was driven to a large rustic building down in the valley. HOTEL BABADAHS it said. It looked like a resort in the Poconos, only there were no front desk, no bellhops, no keys to the rooms. There weren't even locks on the doors.

Jane showed me to the Babadahs Suite. What a joint. I had a sitting room, a private deck, and a kitchenette stocked with carrot juice, granola, sprouts, and tofu patties. In the middle of the enormous bedroom was a waterbed so big you could do laps.

On the wall opposite the bed was a life-size photograph of Sidney looking at me in his strange, new way. And on top of the desk was the local equivalent of the Gideon Bible, *Sayings of the Master,* a picture of Sidney on the cover and behind him, soft-focus, sort of looking over his shoulder, the ghostly face of Babadahs 1.

Off the bedroom was the deck with hot tub and jacuzzi, and off the other side was a sitting room with a library of Babadahs books and a television set and VCR with stacks of Babadahs tapes. "We'll have some of Dad soon," Jane said. I couldn't imagine what they'd be like if Sidney never said anything. Maybe like Andy Warhol's eight-hour movie of the Empire State Building.

There was also a marble bathroom, with complimentary products lined up. Babadahs Hand Lotion, All Natural. Babadahs Shampoo, All Natural. Babadahs Toothpaste, All Natural. Babadahs Soap, All Natural. Everything made from honey and wheat germ and olive oil. In a pinch, you could eat the stuff.

There was a little picture of the old Babadahs on each container and this message: "These products are approved for approaching the Master." I wondered whether they would keep saying this now that Sidney was the Master. Of course, Sidney has allergies too. Maybe allergies are part of the guru shtick, proves they're sensitive or something.

When Jane left, I noticed a placard on the back of the door like the ones they put up in hotels which tell you where the fire exits are. Only this one said:

THREE-FOURTHS OF THE HUMAN RACE WILL BE DEAD OF AIDS BY THE YEAR 2015. ONLY THE ENLIGHTENED WILL SURVIVE. IF YOU HAVE SEX WHILE HERE AS OUR GUEST, OBSERVE ALL MALA RESTRICTIONS AND USE THE MATERIALS IN YOUR BEDSIDE TABLE.

— BABADAHS II

Babadahs II! Already Sidney was coming out with proclamations.

Intrigued, I went to the bedside table. In the drawer was a box of condoms, Babadahs Prophylactics, All Natural. These were no cheap Trenton, New Jersey, condoms either; these were made in Switzerland, of sheep intestines.

Also in the drawer were several pairs of rubber gloves, not the horsey ones for washing dishes but the thin, white ones gynecologists use for internal examinations. Boy, this was some hotel!

Finally, there was a little booklet in the drawer called "Enlightened Sex." It was full of short excerpts from Babadahs' (not my Sidney, the other Babadahs) discourses on yin and yang, positive and negative energy, Tantric sex, ordinary versus cosmic orgasms. An extra page was glued into the back of the booklet dated just a week before and signed "Babadahs II." It said, "Condoms and rubber gloves are now mandatory. Also, because of the world AIDS crisis, oral and anal sex are no longer permitted in the ashram."

But Sidney — oral and anal, two out of three? Mind you, I wasn't asking for myself. I never understood what they were about anyway.

This page went on to say, "Kissing is now strongly discouraged in the ashram. Hug, don't kiss." Sidney was doing away with kissing? In India the Orange People kissed everyone in sight. You couldn't walk across the ashram without getting kissed four or five times by absolute strangers.

Finally, this page said, "Remember: Know Your Sex Partner," like it was the Eleventh Commandment or something. This sure would put a crimp in the Orange People's style. For them, knowing their sex partner would be the equivalent of other people becoming monks. I worried: would Sidney lose his sex-crazed disciples before he half got going? I'd have much preferred his taking up another trade, but if Sidney was going to be a guru, I wanted him to be a success. All this discussion of sex made me long for a bath. I took off my clothes and tried out the jacuzzi and hot tub. Nice. I laid back and relaxed and looked up at that blue desert sky. This was the life. Being the guru's mother had its perks.

I lay down on the waterbed to rest. It was like lying on jello. The bed moved so much I started to get seasick, so I lay very still, hoping it would stop. Somehow I fell asleep and dreamed of men and women wearing nothing but rubber gloves and surgical masks, circling each other in bedrooms like wrestlers.

I AWOKE ten hours later. Bells were tinkling softly somewhere, and the sweetest birds chirped outside in the garden of the hotel. In walked a Ma with breakfast for me: fruits I'd never seen before, a bowl of Babadahs Natural Cereal, and tea which was blood-red in color—made from some root. "Works wonders for getting your energy level up," this Ma said.

She also had a copy for me of the day's *Babadahs Times*, the newspaper published at the ashram. There was a huge picture of Sidney in color and a headline big enough for World War III saying:

BABADAHS ANUDABA BECOMES THE ANOINTED ONE TODAY:
"SLAVE OF SLAVES" BECOMES KING.

At the bottom of the page was a picture of me arriving at Babadahspuram. First time in my life my picture's in the paper and I make the front page!

This Ma looked familiar. My God, it was Ma Prem Isabel, my daughter-in-law. Being so involved with Elaine and the children, I hadn't thought about her for a long time and hadn't recognized her because she looked so tired and worn. Besides, all Orange People look alike.

As we hugged, Isabel sort of palpitated my body. "Hmm," she said, "tight." She offered to tone me up for the big day with a massage.

Why not? I can be as hedonistic as the next person.

Isabel took a massage table out of the closet, and I climbed aboard. She rubbed and I talked. "Do you and Sidney . . . see each other?" I asked, hoping this wouldn't sound too nosey.

For a moment Isabel didn't know who I was talking about; "Sidney" was two names ago. "No," she finally replied. "I was privileged once to be His holy vessel, but now that He is the Babadahs . . . ." Isabel suggested that Sidney didn't have sex anymore in a conventional sense. "He has *become* sex," she said.

"Probably what he always wanted," I joked. Isabel nodded seriously.

After the massage I showered, and while I was in the bathroom Isabel laid out a gorgeous orange robe. It was bordered in red brocade and had red sequins which caught the light every way I turned. Isabel dressed me and brushed my hair. This was better than Helena Rubinstein.

Outside the Hotel Babadahs a Rolls-Royce waited waited for me. In the back was Jane, absolutely lit up with excitement. Also in back was George Smith, like me, invited out for the big day. George was dressed in a robe like mine, which made it easier to believe it about him being a homo. "Well," George said, "what do you think of your son now?"

I confess I didn't know what to think and was grateful when the Rolls glided along the river and I could just smile at George and not answer.

The Rolls took us to this enormous glass building, every pane clear as crystal. It was beautiful, but I hated to think of Sidney's Windex bill. Inside, seated on acres of white linoleum, were thousands of disciples, each with a mala around his neck and, in the lockets, pictures of my Sidney.

Everyone was dressed in their finery. With the sunlight streaming in through the glass all that orange was dazzling, almost blinding.

George, Jane, and I were escorted directly to the front — no sniffing this time — and as we passed between the disciples they craned to see me and a murmur passed among them like a breeze moving through a field of orange flowers: "It's her." I was a celebrity.

We sat on the floor in a reserved place. On one side of us were the press and television cameras. *Life* was there and *People* and *Newsweek* and *Time* and *The Oregonian* and *The New York Times* and CBS and ABC and the BBC and even this man who is writing a book about Sidney. George seemed to know all these people, said they had been interviewing him about Sidney.

On the other side of us was a small orchestra which began to play — not that miserable, droning Indian music but the Beatles. "Lucy in the Sky with Diamonds," they played. Things were sure changing under Sidney's administration.

Everyone got to their feet and danced in place. All these thousands of orange people dancing and laughing. The building shook.

I got up and danced too — what the heck? This delighted everyone around me: the guru's mother herself, dancing.

After a while things quieted down and everyone was seated again. The Om started, but, luckily, didn't go on too long. Outside, an enormous silver Rolls-Royce pulled up, much bigger than the ones I had been riding around in. This one was a custom-made convertible, open to the sky, and in the back, like the president on the way to his inauguration, sat Sidney. The orchestra began to play Cat Stevens' "Morning Has Broken." "Dad's favorite song," Jane whispered.

Sidney entered the building, a tiny figure in a gorgeous white robe fringed with jewels and wearing white gloves. He looked better than the Pope. Down the center aisle he came, staring vacantly ahead, that unearthly look on his face. The flashbulbs of the press lit and lit and lit again, but Sidney didn't blink. People around me oohed and aahed.

Okay, so he had never made full professor. And maybe these orange people were crazy. But they had chosen my Sidney as their guru, and you know what? — I was just going to sit back and enjoy it.

Sidney climbed on to the raised platform up front. It was covered with flowers, except for a spot in the middle occupied by the same throne-like chair I'd seen him in the day before.

Sidney sat down and closed his eyes. He didn't make a sound, didn't scratch, didn't answer questions or preach, just sat there. It was incredibly quiet. It was so quiet my ears hurt.

All those thousands of disciples looked at Sidney, smiles on their faces. They just sat there and watched him.

"What's going on?" I whispered to Jane.

"We're experiencing Dad's aliveness," Jane replied.

Later, I learned this was called *Satsang,* heart-to-heart communication. You stay very still and pick up the guru's vibes. I wasn't picking up any especially, but I enjoyed the effect Sidney had on everyone else.

After forty-five minutes of this, Sidney's expression changed ever so slightly. It could have been gas, but the disciples went crazy. "Too much," someone behind me said.

Good thing Sidney didn't do anything more dramatic. If he'd gotten up and hopped on one foot these people would have keeled over dead from the excitement.

Finally Sidney stood up, put his gloved hands together, and namasted. He namasted to the right, he namasted to the left, then he namasted straight out front. Everyone beamed at him like lasers. You never saw so many teeth.

Now Sidney was coming off the platform. I thought he was leaving, but he walked over to where I was sitting, took my hand, and helped me to my feet. Then, looking me full in the face with that blank stare, before I could protest, he put his right hand on my head and dug his thumb into my forehead, giving his mother the old third-eye treatment.

"Ooooooooooooooh," I cried, not embarrassed, even with three thousand people behind me laughing. Nothing ever felt so good. This was better than sex.

How can I describe it? All the headaches I've ever had were fluttering out of my head at once. All my troubles were suddenly gone. "Sidney," I whispered, "how'd you learn to do this?"

Sidney took me by the hand and led me up onto the platform. I stood there, those thousands of disciples looking up at me. From the folds of his robe Sidney produced a vial with a gold filigree top. It contained an orange substance with the consistency of axle grease. Later, I learned it included some of Babadahs' ashes.

Sidney motioned for me to take this substance and rub it on his face. So I did. I buttered it all over his forehead, his neck, his cheeks. Then Sidney motioned for me to wipe my hands on his beautiful white robe. I didn't want to, but he insisted. A disciple who's a

Hollywood movie star later paid a million dollars for that robe.
Sidney handed me a slip of paper and indicated he wanted me to
read it aloud. "Really?" I said to him. This seemed just like September 21, 1976 or whatever that boy's name is by now. Sidney pointed
to the paper again.

"This stain," I shouted to all that multitude, "is proof of my
imperfection. Let no one make a God out of me. I am here to awak-
en the God in you."

This touched off mumblings throughout the vast hall about Sidney's humility. It gave me gooze bumps.

Motioning me to follow him, Sidney, orange face and all, came
down from the platform and slowly moved out through the disciples, who were now on their feet, entranced and still. He touched
their cheeks, patted their hair, even playfully pulled on their mala
beads. But never did he lose that blank, almost sad, look on his face.

LATER, I SAT with Jane and George on the verandah of the Hotel
Babadahs drinking more of that red root tea I was fast taking a
liking to.

"How did it happen, Jane?" I asked. "Why did they pick Sidney?"
George wanted to know too.

"Well," Jane replied, "they didn't pick him exactly."

Jane told me that when Babadahs was assassinated everyone
assumed the ashram would collapse, the disciples scatter about the
world. No one could take Babadahs' place. Sure, Ma Anand Devora, who handled the day-to-day affairs of the ashram, was a
capable manager; and Swami Prem Dobo, chief of Confucius
Therapy Temple, was thought to be nearly enlightened. But no
one was Babadahs or even close.

A series of incidents pointed to Sidney as the new guru.

First, there were those who said that, as Babadahs lay dying by
the side of the road, it was not the sign of the cross he made over
himself but the letter "A."

"Why would he make the sign of the cross?" Bartho, chief of
ashram transportation, asked at a temple leaders meeting in Moses
House the day after Babadahs' death. "He hated the cross. I tell you,
I was right next to him. It wasn't a cross; it was an 'A.'"

"That's silly," Ma Anand Devora said irritatedly. "He made the cross because he was a martyr." Most of those at the meeting agreed with Devora.

But when they stepped outside after the meeting, they weren't so sure. There, in the late afternoon sky, was a huge, orange "A." It looked as if it had been branded on the sky. It shimmered in the sun like fire.

The orange "A" was easily explained. A skywriting plane belonging to Oregon for Oregonians had made it. That's the group that drops leaflets and writes things like BETTER DEAD THAN ORANGE in the skies over the ashram. This time an Air Babadahs plane had chased it off as it began to spell out a message. Still, it was spooky, that orange "A" floating alone there in the sky.

"Somebody's trying to tell us something," Bartho said.

Two nights later, after more meetings, Ma Anand Devora was sorting through Babadahs' things in the great house when she came across a slip of paper. It had been used by Babadahs as a bookmark in an ancient copy of the *Bhagavad Gita* he had been reading the day of his assassination. On the bookmark, in Babadahs' unmistakable handwriting, was one word: Anudaba.

Anand Devora took the bookmark with her to the next morning's meeting of the temple leaders in Moses House. "Look," she said, holding the piece of paper up for all to see.

This was strange. Sidney was an ordinary member of the ashram. Some of the leaders didn't even know him. Why had Babadahs written "Anudaba" on that slip of paper?

It was decided to meet with Sidney, but Sidney was nowhere to be found. He wasn't in his room. He wasn't at work. Jane told the leaders she hadn't seen her father since just after Babadahs was killed. "He looked strange," Jane said. "Not just horrified like the rest of us; like he had lost his mind."

The leaders fanned out over the ashram looking for Sidney. Hours went by. Then Prem Dobo spotted something.

Standing on Zen Road, looking at the river, he saw a bit of orange in the tall grass of the grove where Babadahs' ashes had been placed on a marble pedestal. "Anyone down there?" he called.

Prem Dobo hiked down the hillside towards the river. When he got to the grove he found Sidney, outstretched on the ground next to the alabaster urn. He had been lying there for days.

"Anudaba," Prem Dobo said, turning Sidney over. Sidney didn't respond. He was dehydrated and filthy. He stared up vacantly at Prem Dobo.

They put Sidney on a stretcher and took him to the infirmary, where he was bathed and fed intravenously. He slept for twenty-four hours.

The leaders were gathered around Sidney's bedside when he awoke. He opened his eyes and they knew. Sidney was no longer the same person. Lying on the ground next to Babadahs' ashes, he had somehow become a holy man. You could feel it coming off him without him saying a word.

So no one picked Sidney as guru. From that moment on he simply *was* the guru. He'd lost his ego, become enlightened. The word was passed for all disciples to gather at sunrise the next day outside the infirmary for a momentous announcement.

Before sunrise bells began ringing and, in near darkness, the orange people made their way from all corners of the ashram to the infirmary. On the slope outside they stood in clusters, whispering, apprehensive. As the sun broke over the hills, the leaders, like cardinals emerging from the Sistine Chapel after choosing a pope, stepped outside the infirmary door. Ma Anand Devora announced, "I bring you great joy. We have a Master."

The thousands of disciples fell to their knees on the rocky ground as Sidney, clothed in white, walked slowly out of the infirmary and stood among them. He stared out over the multitudes and raised his arms.

Jane was there that morning. "I nearly fainted when I saw it was Dad," she said. "But, of course, it wasn't Dad anymore. It was someone . . . something . . . else."

Sidney stood there, not saying a word. Just stood there blessing everyone, and then he stepped into a Rolls-Royce and was driven to the great house on the hill.

The fact that Sidney didn't say anything—and hasn't said one word since—was at first disquieting to the disciples, who were used to Babadahs' eloquence. Of course, now it's believed Sidney may even be holier than Babadahs, silence being the highest form of communication.

A FEW DAYS LATER I went to see Sidney to say goodbye. George Smith and I were flying back to New York together. George had to get back; he'd just been named Chairman of the English Department at Rutgers.

I walked down that long corridor in Sidney's residence and found him seated in his great chair. "I'm leaving, Sidney" I said. "I have to go home."

Sidney just looked at me, expressionless. As usual he didn't say anything. But as I looked into his eyes I could see he wanted me to stay. It would be a comfort to have his mother around. It was lonely at the top.

I started thinking: Why *do* I have to go home? Who says I have to go home? In New York there would be nothing for me but retirement all alone; the senior citizens club, a nursing home someday. Not to mention having to constantly answer questions about my son the guru. It had been bad enough when he was just a disciple; people thought he was a bit crazy. But now? With Sidney soon to be on the cover of *People* magazine?

Here I don't have to answer questions. Here I am somebody, I have, a position: the guru's mother. Jane needs me and, in his own way, Sidney does too. Besides, what if they try to kill Sidney too? I couldn't live with myself if something happened to Sidney and I hadn't stayed here to protect him somehow. I'm still his mother.

So I decided to stay—for a while, anyway. They gave me a little house on the hillside, and Jane lives with me. We have a beautiful view of the river and the hills beyond.

When I told George Smith I wouldn't be flying back with him he smiled, but he had a wistful look on his face. It was as if he envied me.

Elaine got real mad at me when I didn't come home. Naturally. I'd have gotten mad at me too if I was her. Elaine thought I'd gone over totally to the other side.

I haven't. Somebody gave me a mala with Sidney's picture, but I keep it in my underwear drawer. I wear orange sometimes because that's all you can buy here, but I'm not Sidney's disciple. Even if I wanted to be I couldn't. I'm his mother.

Now, as it turns out, Elaine is glad I'm here. She had a big fight with Harry and my grandson is coming out for a visit. Elaine wants me to keep him away from Sidney, make sure he doesn't become a disciple too. "Mildred," Elaine cries to me over the phone, "if it happens to Harry too I'll just die."

I tell Elaine not to worry. But *I'm* worried. I mean, what is this? We're normal people, we're just like everyone else. Why is my only granddaughter a member of a cult? Why is my son the "god" of the cult? What if Harry ever *does* become a disciple? What am *I* doing here?

I'll tell you one reason I'm here: Where else can a seventy-two-year-old woman get, gratis, instant relief from all aches and pains just by having someone dig his thumb into her forehead? Beats Midicare, I'll tell you.

Also, this isn't India. You can get anything you want at the ashram; there's restaurants, movies, boutiques. In India you couldn't even get Tab.

Living at the ashram is like being on permanent vacation. It's a cruise ship, a summer camp, God's own Club Med. Who knows what may happen if one of the older swamis takes a fancy to me? I have this orange negligee you wouldn't believe. I could get used to the rubber gloves.

I get to see Sidney every day during his drive-by. He sits there, his hand raised in blessing, looking like Buddha. Everybody goes crazy as he passes by.

There's a lot more security during the drive-by these days. A helicopter overhead, spotters on every hillside. Some say we have machine-gun nests up there.

Usually Jane is beside me at the drive-by. Sidney blesses us both—but not any different from the way he blesses everyone along the road. The expression never changes on his face. The disciples believe Sidney is the New Age incarnation of God.

Maybe he is and maybe he isn't. Maybe he just went completely crazy lying there by Babadahs' ashes for three days.

Or maybe he just likes being a guru more than he liked being an English professor. Sometimes I think I see a little smile in the corner of his mouth as he goes by, a smile just for me. Others would say it isn't there, but I see it. It's as if Sidney is saying, "Hey, Mom, do you believe this? Me, Sidney, the guru?"

Yesterday, as he drove by, blessing all of us standing there in the dusty road, I leaned into the window and said, "*Zei gesund,* Sidney. As long as you're happy."

COLOPHON

A Bliss Case was designed by Allan Kornblum, using the Ventura Publisher book design program. The text is set in Bem, a version of the great classical face, Bembo, designed by Francesco Griffo for the most influential Venetian printer of the late Renaissance, Aldus Manutius. The type was run off by the highly cooperative Stanton Publication Services. This book was printed on acid-free paper, and smyth sewn into wrappers for added durability.

is book was published by Coffee House Press, a
all independent publisher of exciting contempo-
y literature. The Coffee House Press list includes
on by W. P. Kinsella, Maxine Chernoff, Andrei
rescu, Keith Abbott, and Rochelle Ratner, and
ry by Ed Sanders, Cid Corman, Anne Waldman,
Clark and Faye Kicknosway. Coffee House also
uces the Morning Coffee Chapbooks, a series
eautiful letterpress poetry pamphlets. All of
e books are printed on acid-free paper with
bindings, and are designed to be durable as
as attractive and entertaining.

u would like to learn more about the books
ished by Coffee House, fill out this card and
it to the press. You will receive catalogs in-
ing you of forthcoming titles, and the staff
be happy to answer any questions you may
. And ask about other Coffee House Press titles
ving at your favorite bookstore.

e _____

ress _____

of this book _____

e purchased _____